DREAM WEAVERS

NIGHT OF THE SCARY FAIRIES

To all those who bring magic into my life
– AS

For every dreamer, big or small, all around the world
– FB

LITTLE TIGER
An imprint of Little Tiger Press Limited
1 Coda Studios, 189 Munster Road, London SW6 6AW

Imported into the EEA by Penguin Random House Ireland,
Morrison Chambers, 32 Nassau Street, Dublin D02 YH68

A paperback original
First published in Great Britain in 2023

Text copyright © Annabelle Sami, 2023
Illustrations copyright © Forrest Burdett, 2023

ISBN: 978-1-78895-600-0

MIX
Paper | Supporting
responsible forestry
FSC® C171272

The Forest Stewardship Council® (FSC®) is a global, not-for-profit organization
dedicated to the promotion of responsible forest management worldwide. FSC defines
standards based on agreed principles for responsible forest stewardship that are supported
by environmental, social, and economic stakeholders. To learn more, visit www.fsc.org

10 9 8 7 6 5 4 3 2 1

DREAM WEAVERS

NIGHT OF THE SCARY FAIRIES

ANNABELLE SAMI

ILLUSTRATED BY
FORREST BURDETT

LITTLE TIGER

LONDON

WARNING!

Top-secret information for the eyes
of Soothsayers only.

The following knowledge has been gathered
and protected by generations.

And now it falls to you.

Use it wisely.

CHAPTER ONE
FIRST-DAY JITTERS

The first thing I notice is my bare feet. I've always thought they were weird because my second toe is longer than my big toe. Everyone knows the big toe is supposed to be the biggest. I mean, it's in the name.

Then I notice the cold grass poking up between my weird long toe and the big one. Odd. It's night-time, so I'm wearing my Spider-Man pyjamas. But why am I on a clifftop with frosty wind rushing through my hair? And where even am I?

I look out at the night sky stretching
before me and gasp at the vivid colours. It's
streaked with neon green and swirls of violet,
all lit up by bright stars. It almost hurts my
eyes to look but I can't turn away.

Gradually, from the edge of my awareness,
I notice a sound. It's a bit like children
giggling and it's coming from down low, in
the grass. I stoop to get a closer look and
realize that the field is full of tiny, glowing

figures! They're dancing around, flitting back and forth on delicate wings that beat so fast they look blurred. Fear creeps up my spine as I back away when, suddenly, one of the tiny figures springs forwards. In one movement its small mouth opens and it *chomps* down on my big toe.

"*Ouch!*"

★

My eyes fly open to the sound of my alarm clock and my dog licking my face.

"OK, OK! Good morning, Rupert." I laugh, gently pushing away his furry snout. "It's weird… I've had the same dream now for two days. Maybe I'm nervous about school starting back. What do you think?"

Rupert cocks his head to one side as if to say, "Why are you asking me?" Then he springs off the bed and races out of the room. People always joke that me and Rupert could be brothers, since we have the same curly light brown hair and big round eyes. Although I would be worried if my real brother had a tail…

I hear Rupert thunder down the stairs and into the kitchen where Mama is already bustling about. Breakfast time in our house means two things: the smell of sizzling butter and the sound of classical music. My mama is Italian and she *loves* Italian opera (she'll sometimes listen to German opera too if she's feeling extra dramatic). She even gave Rupert the middle name Poochini so he'd "remember his Italian roots". (I don't ever point out that Rupert's breed is *Australian* labradoodle.)

It's the first day back at school after the summer holidays so I drag myself out of bed, not used to getting up early again yet. When I finally get dressed and walk into the kitchen, Mama is frying eggs and holding Roberto, my baby brother, on one hip.

"Morning, Mama. Morning, Berto."
I give them both a kiss.

"Buongiorno, Tito," Mama sings. "Eat! Eat! Mum is going to take you to school in fifteen minuti."

I peer out of the kitchen window and spot my mum working in her shed at the bottom of the garden. I call them Mama and Mum so we don't get confused but really my parents

11

couldn't be more different. My mum is DIY obsessed and loves working on random projects. Our house is a happy mix of hand-made furniture, Mama's opera posters and records, a squeaky staircase and a well-stocked kitchen.

As I eat my eggs, a little flutter of nerves rises up in my stomach but I do my best to push them back down. I'm in Year Five now! It seems silly to be nervous about school.

After a hearty breakfast I grab my school bag and head out into the garden to find Mum. She's in her shed, completely absorbed in finding the perfect rivet in a box of loose screws.

"Oh, Tito! Time to go already?" she says, finally noticing me. She grabs her keys from a hook on the wall and we make our way to the car.

I don't say anything when we get in, I'm too focused on keeping the nerves at bay. But Mum knows something is up.

"You got first-day jitters?" she asks, reaching out to pat my leg.

I don't want to talk about it so I just say, "I had a strange dream."

"Well, you're probably just a bit nervous about going into a new year. Like Mama always says, you are sensitive."

I cringe a little bit at that word. "Maybe."

Sometimes I wish I wasn't so sensitive. It's a

new year at school but it's not like anything's changed. I've had the same classmates since Reception and my best friends Tiffany and Murray will still be there. We've been BFFs our whole lives. We went to nursery together, caught chickenpox at the same time, star in every nativity as the three wise men and now we're at the same primary school.

This summer was one of our best yet. We spent *every day* together, (apart from when Tiff was rehearsing for the local theatre group play and Murray was at football practice). We built a shelter out of massive branches near the river in the woods and hung out there. Murray and I went to watch Tiff perform on the opening night of her play and she was *really* good. I even managed to convince Tiff to come and watch one of Murray's matches and we shouted so much that I lost my voice.

But now it's September. The new school

year came round quickly.

My tummy lurches again and I know for sure that I'm nervous.

Everything at school will be the same, I tell myself. At least, I hope it is. I've never liked surprises.

★

When I walk into my Year Five classroom it's buzzing with the excitement of different haircuts, brand-new stationery and tales from the holidays.

"Tito, over here!" Tiff shouts, waving to me from the back of the class.

"Nice glasses, Tiff," I say, admiring the green frames.

Tiffany smiles and wiggles her eyebrows. "Thanks! I saw the lead singer of 2True wearing them so I *had* to get some just like it."

"They remind me of snot," Murray says.

"Murray!" Tiffany and I shout, before cracking up laughing. When you've known Murray for as long as we have, you learn he isn't being rude. Murray just says exactly what he's thinking and sometimes it comes across a bit … blunt.

The classroom door creaks open and Ms Branberry, our class tutor, walks in carrying an impossibly tall stack of books. Next to her is a girl I've never seen before.

"A new girl," Tiffany whispers in awe. We haven't had a new student join the class since Year One!

"Hi, Year Five!" Ms Branberry says loudly. "I'm so happy to be your form tutor this year and even happier that we have a new student joining us!"

I like Ms Branberry but she does get excited about *everything*.

"Now our new student is called –" Ms Branberry gestures to the girl to introduce herself, but the girl's cheeks go pink and she stays quiet so our teacher continues. "Her name is Neena and she has just moved here from Chitral in Pakistan. Who has heard of Pakistan?"

A few people put their hands up, including me. I watched a documentary about Pakistan with my mum. Travel shows are our favourite.

Ms Branberry scans the class and her eyes settle on me. Uh-oh.

"Tito, since you have your hand up and because I know you are a very sensible boy, would you look after Neena today?"

I mean … I can't really say no, can I?
I want Ms Branberry to like me and I don't
want to upset Neena. I force a smile and nod
but my stomach is churning. I was already
nervous and now I have to speak to a new
kid. I can't remember the last time I spoke
to someone new. Our town's so small that
everyone knows each other.

"Thank you, Tito," Ms Branberry beams,
ushering Neena to sit next to me. "We want
Neena to feel extremely welcome here so
I expect everyone to be *very*, *very* kind to
her. OK?"

"Yes, Ms Branberry," we reply as one.

Neena scuttles over to our table at the
back and sits on the empty chair next to me.
I try not to stare at her but I notice she keeps
her eyes down the whole time. If *I'm* feeling
nervous about the first day back, then Neena
must feel even worse, being completely new.

Come on, Tito, be brave. I'm sure she doesn't bite.

I take a deep breath and ignore the uneasy churning in my belly. Ms Branberry has trusted me to look after the new girl so I'm going to do my best to make her feel welcome.

I can feel Tiffany and Murray's eyes on me as the class starts chatting about their summer holidays again. They want me to say something to Neena.

"So…" I begin, turning to look at the new girl. "When did you move here?"

Neena opens her mouth but then quickly looks away and starts rummaging around in her backpack.

I try again. "Uh… Did your parents move here for a job?"

Neena doesn't reply but pulls out a leatherbound black notebook.

I can feel my palms start to get clammy. I need backup! I turn to Tiff and Murray and mouth "help" with wide eyes.

"Neeeeeeeennaaaaa," Tiffany sings, her pigtail bunches bobbing as she warbles up and down a scale. "What bands do you like?"

I jump in to explain the singing. "In case you haven't guessed, Tiffany loves performing. She's going to be a pop star one day!"

"Um, pop *icon*," Tiffany corrects me, and busts out some moves right there at the desk.

I watch Neena's face for a reaction, *anything* to show she's feeling more comfortable. She gives us a small smile and then immediately looks back down at the pages of her notebook. Her wavy dark hair falls in front of her face like a curtain.

I try again. "This is Murray. He's the best rugby player in our school. Actually, he's the best at every kind of sport."

Murray squints at Neena. "Maybe she doesn't speak English."

Eeeeek. Murray's habit of saying whatever's in his head is *not* helpful right now.

Neena looks up, turns to Murray and Tiff and says, "Hi. Nice to meet you." Then she goes back to her notebook.

"OK, progress," Murray says, clapping his hands together.

Tiff whacks him on the arm.

They begin bickering in the way they often do, like brother and sister. I can't help but feel a little deflated… Neena didn't say hi to me. But I won't give up just yet. She can't go a *whole day* without speaking, can she?

★

I'm pretty sure Neena hates me. It's the last lesson of the day and she *still* hasn't spoken to me. I hope I haven't done anything to upset her. In my head I run through my attempts to get her to speak. I told her my best Mum jokes and offered her some of my pesto gnocchi at lunch. I even joined in with Tiffany's lunchtime performance as a backing dancer to make her laugh. But she didn't crack a smile! She just sat and wrote in her notebook, her fingers anxiously fiddling with the spine. I feel like I've failed.

In maths, I try to focus on equations but the numbers keep going fuzzy on the page and my eyes droop. Being back at school is tiring enough without trying to help a new student settle in.

Then there's a sudden ruckus at the back of the class and my eyes fly open.

A chair falls to the floor with a clang. I whirl round and am shocked to see Leonard and Harry, hands flapping in front of them, in the middle of a fight!

"Oh my gosh," Tiffany gasps.

"I can't believe it," I whisper. "They're usually so quiet."

"They're not even fighting properly, they're too small," Murray says, a bit too loudly.

Leonard and Harry slap each other's hands in a messy rumble, their faces bright red.

Ms Branberry rushes to the back of the class, yelling, "Boys! Stop!" She pulls Leonard and Harry apart and stares at them, her mouth agape. This fight has sent her into a *whole new level* of dramatics.

"I cannot believe what I'm seeing," she shrieks. "Both of you to the head teacher's office NOW."

Leonard and Harry sulkily troop out of the room.

I agree with Ms Branberry. I can't believe it either. They're best friends! And Leonard is Head of Year for goodness' sake. He's the best-behaved boy in the school.

No one can concentrate for the rest of the afternoon, and when the school bell finally rings, Neena quickly packs up her belongings and rushes out into the playground. Ms Branberry watches her leave and then beckons me over to her desk.

"Neena seems to be struggling to settle in…" she says, tapping the table with her pencil.

My heart sinks. "I know, I'm sorry. I tried everything I could. Maybe she needs more time?"

I feel like I've let both her and Neena down.

"Could you keep an eye on her for the rest of the week?" Ms Branberry asks.

I nod quickly, happy to have a second chance.

"Great." Ms Branberry lowers her glasses and peers at me over the top. "I'm counting on you."

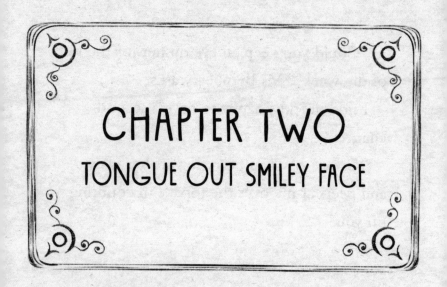

CHAPTER TWO
TONGUE OUT SMILEY FACE

"Berto, you must eat two more carrot sticks per favore," Mama instructs, pointing to my brother's plate.

"Na uh!" Berto pouts, pushing it away from him.

Me and Mum catch each other's eye and try not to giggle. Roberto and Mama have an ongoing dinner battle because he refuses to eat vegetables.

"Look, Berto, Tito loves the carrots!" Mum says enthusiastically, gesturing to my spoon.

I play along, taking a big spoonful of minestrone soup with carrots in it and slurping loudly. "Mmmmmmmmmmm," I say, rubbing my tummy. I'm really selling it.

Berto just looks at me and sticks out his tongue.

"Mio dio, I give up," Mama sighs. "Tito, how was your first day back, amore?"

I can't help but sigh when I think about the day.

"That bad?" Mum says, raising an eyebrow.

"Well, Ms Branberry asked me to look after this new girl – she's moved here from Pakistan – but she didn't speak to me all day. She just looked really sad. I don't know what to do to help."

Mama reaches out and squeezes my hand. "Ahhhh, there's my sensitivo boy, always trying to help others."

I roll my eyes. "I'm not sensitivo, Mama.

27

I just want to do a good job because the teacher asked me to."

"When your mama came to the UK she was very homesick," Mum jumps in. "I tried to learn everything I could about Milan so I could talk to her about her hometown. It helped Mama feel better. Maybe Neena is homesick too?"

Mama nods along. "That's a buona idea. It helps to have something in common."

I mull this over as I finish my soup.
It couldn't hurt to learn a bit more about
where Neena comes from and it might make
her open up to me. I don't like to admit it
but my parents are usually right about this
sort of thing.

Once dinner is over, I ask Mum to log me
on to the computer in her home office and
open up Google.

I wrack my brain to remember where
Ms Branberry had said Neena was from.
After a few unsuccessful spelling attempts,
I finally find "Chitral – Pakistan" and load
the image results. There are open mountain
ranges, dotted with green shrubbery, hills
with a valley running through the middle and
the sparkling Chitral River surrounded by
green farmland.

I decide to go back to the web search
results and scroll down, opening the
Wikipedia page. It has lots of general facts

about the town, but I don't think that telling Neena the population of Chitral is just under 50,000 will cure her homesickness.

I scroll for a while before something catches my eye. It's an article called "Top Ten Chitrali Mythological Beasts".

The region of Chitral is rich in folklore and myth. Many of the creatures that people told stories about years ago are still very much alive in the hearts of Chitrali people today. Here are some of our favourite beasts that are said to roam the mountains and valleys of Chitral.

My heart beats faster but I carry on reading. I remind myself that the website says "mythological" so even if these so-called beasts are scary, I know they aren't real.

Night Demons
Hellhounds

Fire Giants

Ghoul Horses

My mouth goes dry and I pull the curtains
closed so I can't see the blackness outside.
The air seems to chill around me.

"They aren't real, Tito," I scold myself.

But as I read on, I'm properly scared.
Just the descriptions of the fairies and pixies
said to live in the tallest mountain make my
palms start sweating. I *hate* scary stuff. Mama
said she couldn't even read *The Gruffalo* to me
as a baby because I would cry.

There's a knock on the door and I literally
jump out my seat.

"Oh sorry, love, I didn't mean to scare
you! It's time for bed," Mum says. She's in
her dressing gown, a sleep mask perched
on her forehead. I look at the time and it's
already 10 p.m.!

Tiredness prickles at my eyes but when

I get myself cosy and tucked in, my mind is still buzzing with Chitrali folklore. I think that Mama's right: I am *sensitivo*.

I shake my head as if it will help the thoughts disappear and try to imagine fluffy bunnies and rainbows. At least now I know some stuff about Chitral so I can talk to Neena tomorrow.

Tomorrow...

To...

mor...

row...

★

I feel cold grass under the soles of my feet. *Huh? Haven't I been here before?* Looking up, the sky is soaked with colour: purple, green and blue.

I take a few shaky steps along the clifftop towards some towering pine trees. They're huddled together, as if they're scared too.

As I get closer, a horrible buzzing noise rises from the branches and a cloud of tiny red glowing figures fly out from behind the trees. They swarm like angry bees, and they're coming right at me!

Run, Tito. Run.

I beg my legs to move but I can't feel them any more and I stay rooted to the spot. The red figures fly closer and I can just make out their small heads topped with spiky hair, two spindly arms and two legs.

"Do you know Neena? She is so *rude*," one of them hisses.

"You should avoid her. A horrible girl," another says, whizzing past my head.

"No, she's just shy!" I shout back at them.

"So you *do* know her," one of them says, sharing a sly smile with the rest of the pack. "She goes to your school?"

"Yes, and I'm not going to avoid her. That would be mean," I say, standing my ground.

"Maybe you *are* mean," two of the figures say in unison. "Maybe you're cruel and nasty."

I shake my head. "No. No, I'm not!"

I try to catch a glimpse of the figures in better detail but they're so fast and they zip off in different directions.

"Don't trust Neena. She's bad news," a voice says, somewhere behind me.

"Mean and nasty Tito…" another voice hisses, buzzing past me.

Beep, beep, beep, beep.

"Bad. News."

Beep, beep, beep, beep.

Beep, beep, beep, beep.

I wake up with my eyes still closed and feel the sheets around me damp with sweat. After a moment in the darkness, I reach out and turn off the beeping alarm clock.

Ugh, what a horrible dream.

Four paws thunder up the stairs so I brace myself for Rupert who jumps up, landing on my tummy.

"Oof, good morning, Rupes. I had a weird dream… It was in the same place as my dream last night. But there were these weird creatures. They were talking about Neena."

Rupert gently nudges me with his nose before bounding away. I think he's bored of hearing about my dreams.

"Tito! *Andiamo!* I have to drop you off early today," Mama calls up the stairs.

I rub my eyes. School! My mind feels so muddled from the dream that I almost forgot. I stretch out my arms and roll my shoulders, hearing one of them click satisfyingly.

It's time to re-enter the world of the waking.

★

As soon as I walk into registration and see Neena sitting at our desk, my heart beats faster. That weird dream is still swirling in my head. What if those things were true? Is Neena really bad news? As I sit down in my seat, Neena looks up but I turn away. I won't be mean, that's not me … but I might avoid her, just until I get my thoughts together.

I manage to keep this up for a while – it turns out getting your thoughts together takes longer than I expected.

Throughout morning classes I don't say a word to Neena, and I even form a group of three with Murray and Tiffany for geography so I don't have to work with her. But when lunchtime rolls around and I see her sitting alone in the dining hall I immediately feel sick with guilt. Murray has rugby practice and Tiff is auditioning for the winter concert, so I'm the only person who she knows.

It was just a stupid dream, I tell myself as I approach her table. *Don't be a meanie.*

Neena is drawing in her notebook so I sit down next to her and try to look friendly. I'm not sure it's working.

"Hey, Neena, sorry we haven't spoken much today," I say, twiddling my thumbs.

She stops scribbling and looks up at me. For the first time I notice that she has very bright green eyes. She looks quite magical, like some sort of superhero.

"Um, I did some reading about Chitral last night. It's really pretty. It kind of reminded me of this place in the mountains in northern Italy, near where my mama's from. I mean they're not *that* similar, unless you speak Italian in Pakistan…" I laugh awkwardly because I realize I've started rambling. I pause and take a breath, giving Neena time to respond.

Slowly Neena smiles. Just a little. "Yes, the mountains in Chitral are very beautiful," she says in a quiet, husky voice.

I feel my shoulders relax and warmth spread through my chest. She *was* homesick, just like Mama and Mum said.

"I looked at lots of pictures," I carry on, not wanting the conversation to end. "You must miss it. Do the rest of your family still live there?"

Neena's smile quickly fades and her eyes move back to her notebook.

No! Quick, go back to talking about Chitral.

"Yeah, so I uh, learned about the geography and the people. Oh, and I read some really freaky folktales that I think gave me nightma—"

"Nightmares?" Neena says suddenly. "What kind of folktales did you read?"

Now she thinks I'm a wuss. I shouldn't

have mentioned the nightmares.

"Um, I read about different types of creatures, like there was something called a … hellhound, I think?" I try to act casual, like the painting of the wolf-like beast isn't etched into my memory (probably) for ever.

Neena grins and flips open her notebook, searching through the pages eagerly. She finds the page she was looking for and jabs her finger on a sketch.

"Here, like this?" she asks, pointing at a wolfy-looking creature. There are words written above it too but they're in a language I don't understand. "You must think this is all very strange…"

Neena suddenly seems a bit shy again and her brown cheeks have gone slightly pink.

"No I don't!" I reassure her. "It's not weird, it's interesting. Did you draw that wolf? It's very good!"

Neena's drawing is realistic enough to make me feel a bit scared again.

She nods and starts flipping through the sketchbook showing me the other drawings she's done.

"I love the folklore of my hometown. There are so many amazing creatures. We call them jinn. They are like spirits."

Neena's eyes light up as she talks me through various other sketches. She's a completely different person to the shy girl I met yesterday. But as she flicks past one particular page I see an image that looks familiar. I reach out and hold the page open, my eyes fixed on the drawing of many tiny figures, clustered together in a group.

"What are those?" I say quietly, trying to work out where I've seen them before.

"Those are *paris*," Neena replies, and I can feel her eyes studying me.

"What are puh-rees?" I repeat, trying to pronounce the word the same way she did.

"I think in English you call them … fairies," Neena says.

Something clicks in my memory and I realize where I've seen the figures before. "This is going to sound so weird, but I think I dreamed of something like this. They looked a bit different, though. One of them bit me on the toe! It felt so real…"

Neena slams the book shut, making me

jump, then she looks directly into my eyes. "You saw them in a dream?"

I nod.

"And you remember this dream clearly? Like it was real?"

"Um, yes and yes." I feel a bit silly for mentioning it.

She thinks for a minute then tears out a blank page from her notebook and hands it to me with a pencil.

"I want you to draw a symbol on this page," she instructs me. "Any symbol. Whatever comes into your head."

I hesitate before picking up the pencil. What's going on? Neena's mood has changed so quickly. I wonder if this is a game she used to play at her old school? I want her to keep opening up to me so I draw an image on the page.

Neena looks at it and screws up her nose. "What is it?"

I suppress a giggle. I've drawn the tongue out smiley face emoji. Neena had become so serious that I wanted to lighten the mood. To explain the drawing I poke my tongue out and mimic the  drawing. Thankfully, Neena laughs too.

"OK, this is good," she says, composing herself. "Now I want you to draw this symbol on your hand before you go to sleep.

Huh?

I must look *very* puzzled, because Neena takes a deep breath. "I can't explain. I don't know if I can trust you yet. But make sure you set your alarm clock for the morning.

I will see you later…"

She gathers up her belongings and takes
off so quickly I wonder if I'd imagined it.
I really want to tell Tiffany and Murray
about everything but something tells me
I should keep it a secret. I want to give
Neena a chance to explain, for the symbol
to make sense. I look down at the piece of
paper with the tongue out smiley face on it
and sigh.

What does it mean?

CHAPTER THREE
YOU'RE A DREAMWEAVER!

That evening my tummy starts making weird gurgling sounds. I'm not hungry – I can't be after two portions of Mama's mushroom risotto. But the nearer it gets to bedtime the louder it rumbles. I make up an excuse about needing to finish some homework and go to my room so I can think.

I lie on the carpet looking up at the glow-in-the-dark stars on my ceiling.

Why is this symbol thing making me so nervous? I mean, it's no big deal – I just need to draw it on my hand and go to sleep.

It's not like anything's going to happen.

I jump up and grab a pen. "Here goes!"

I carefully draw the symbol on my hand, turn out the light and crawl into bed. I'm dozing off, under the green glow of the fluorescent stars, when I remember I haven't set my alarm. I quickly turn it on for 7 a.m. then settle back down.

Thoughts drift into my mind as I close my eyes. I remember the way Neena's face lit up when I started speaking about Chitral and I feel happy all over again. I hope I've made a new friend.

Then slowly…

Gently…

I fall—

*

A cold breeze whips me in the face and I smell pine trees. I look around and immediately recognize the clifftop but it seems different this time. Everything is more vivid: the stars in the sky and the brightness of the colours that swirl around in it. The breeze blows again and I feel the hairs on my arms prick up.

I scan the grass for any trace of the glowing figures that had taunted me before but thankfully there's no sign of them. *Phew.*

Just when I think I'm alone, I hear a voice, far away...

Is it... Is it calling my name?

"Tito!"

I turn round and look towards the edge of the cliff, where the sound is coming from. A figure is running towards me.

"Neena!?" I shout.

"Tito!" she beams, as she gets closer. "I knew it! I'm so happy I can trust you. I thought I wouldn't have anyone here to talk to. I thought I would have to stay away from everyone and keep everything secret but..."

She stops in front of me, panting. "You're a Dreamweaver!" She beams, holding her arms out in triumph.

"I'm a … what?" I splutter, very confused. "A dream beaver?"

Neena bursts out laughing. "No. A Dream*weaver*. I had a feeling you might be because you remembered your dream with the paris so clearly. I haven't seen any here yet, though… That must have been a one-off."

I feel like cold water has been splashed over me and my eyes open wide. "Wait! I'm dreaming? How are you here? Where are we?" I look around frantically, taking in my surroundings. It feels as if I'm seeing them for the first time.

Neena nods slowly. "It's kind of like you're awake *in* a dream. And I am too. This is really me, here with you. I'm a Dreamweaver too."

My legs suddenly feel weak and I sit down in the damp grass. I realize that I'm wearing my Spider-Man pyjamas, and now I've probably got a big wet patch on the bum. I *really* wish I was wearing something a bit cooler. Neena's wearing loose, baggy trousers and a dark purple top. She looks very cool, like an explorer or a superhero in a comic book.

"You can ask me questions if you want," says Neena, looking down at me with an amused smile.

"Um, ah, well… What exactly *is* a

Dreamweaver?" I stammer. "I don't think we've learned about them at school."

"You won't have, no," Neena says, holding out her hand. "Follow me."

She pulls me up and towards the small forest of pine trees.

"Nice dream by the way," Neena says over her shoulder. "Very beautiful."

"Uh, thanks," I reply, not quite sure what's going on.

Neena reaches the edge of the forest and turns to face me. "A Dreamweaver can control dreams, create amazing worlds and explore their own mind. It takes some practice but…"

Neena looks at a branch of the tree and holds out her hands, palms up. The air above the branch starts looking wavy and a shape begins to form. Two legs appear first, then a beak and a wing, until a fully formed brown sparrow sits on the branch. Only — "What is that?" I gawp. Above the sparrow's beak is a long, curly black moustache. When the bird chirps, the ends of the moustache curl up, making me laugh out loud.

"It's a dream — anything is possible!" Neena giggles, watching the sparrow. "Why make something that already exists?"

She has a point.

"Come on!" Neena says, running further into the forest. I chase after her and watch in amazement as flowers spring up under her feet. A rush of excitement spreads through my body and I run even faster, caught up in the thrill of the discovery. Neena is standing next to the gnarled stump of a tree, concentrating hard. The air goes wavy again but this time a long, cylindrical shape appears, standing upright on the tree stump. It takes a minute before I realize what it is.

"A HOT DOG?" I cry out, immediately collapsing into a fit of giggles.

Two googly eyes pop up on the sausage, along with a mouth. The hot dog opens its mouth wide and takes a deep breath.

"Laa, la, laaaaaaaaaaaaaaaaaaaaaaaa!" It bellows out a note in a wobbly, operatic voice.

Neena and I fall to our knees laughing, holding our stomachs. When the hot dog finally finishes its dramatic song, I turn to Neena and shake my head in disbelief.

"Is this … *magic?*"

Neena nods at me, smiling.

"And *I* can control dreams too?" I ask, still trying to wrap my mind around it.

"Yes. With practice. Dreamweavers can enter the dreams of other people too. That's how I'm here." Neena holds up her hand where she has drawn my symbol. "To enter the dream of another Dreamweaver, you must know their symbol. If they aren't a Dreamweaver, you just need to hold an item of theirs when you sleep."

I look down at my own hand where I've drawn the tongue out smiley face and groan. "*Why* did I choose this emoji instead of something cool?"

Neena laughs and the smile fades from her face. "Tito. Now you know about Dreamweaving, you *must* keep it a secret. Especially your symbol. There are some people – some Dreamweavers – who use their gift for evil. Keep your symbol safe so they can't enter your dream."

I feel a lump form in my throat. Evil? I've only just started having fun and already Neena is talking about danger. The nervous feeling I'd had in my tummy all evening returns and I suddenly feel out of my depth.

"I'm not sure, Neena, maybe this isn't for me. You don't know me that well yet but … I'm not a very adventurous person," I explain. "In fact, I can be quite a scaredy-cat. Maybe I can't be a Dreamweaver."

Neena takes my hand and looks at me with laser focus. "Tito. You *are* a Dreamweaver – you were born one. Only certain people have this gift. You must have a huge imagination, a belief in the impossible and, most importantly, feel emotions very strongly."

I consider that description while the moustached sparrow squawks nearby.

"I think… I think I have all those things,"
I say finally, not wanting to sound boastful.

The sparrow keeps on squawking.

"Then you are a Dreamweaver," Neena
says gently.

Squawk, squawk, squawk.

A thought pops into my mind. "You said
there are other Dreamweavers… Do you
know them? What about your parents or
siblings?"

Neena's expression darkens for a moment
but then she shakes her head. "That's enough
for tonight, I think you're about to wake up.
I'll see you tomorrow, Tito."

Squawk, squawk, squawk.

Beep, Beep, Beep.

I wake up abruptly and sit bolt upright
in bed, my alarm ringing out loudly next to
me. I'm too dazed to reach out and turn it
off. A dim light melts in through the curtains
and slowly I realize I'm back in my room.

I'm not dreaming any more.

Rupert rushes up the stairs and runs into my bedroom. He stops in surprise to see me awake, already sitting up in bed.

"It's OK, Rupes. Come here," I say groggily, patting the bed. Rupert jumps on happily and starts licking my face.

"I had the freakiest dream last night," I tell him, dodging licks to my nose. "At least, I *think* it was a dream. It felt real…"

Rupert sits back and looks at me with big eyes, before settling down to sleep on the end of my bed.

"I know, I know, even more dream chat,

56

I'm sorry." I laugh, stroking his soft head.

I get ready for school but as I put on my uniform I can't stop thinking about the dream.

Was it real?

★

As I'm walking through the school gates someone runs up behind me and taps me on the shoulder. I whirl round and there's Neena, buzzing with excitement.

"Hey, Dreamweaver," she says quietly.

"So it *was* real!" *I knew it!*

"Yes! How do you feel?" Neena looks at me intensely and I see a flicker of concern in her eyes.

"It's a lot to think about," I say honestly. "I feel a bit scared and sleepy, very sleepy."

"I felt tired too, when I first started dreamweaving," Neena reassures me. "As you get more practice you learn how to wake yourself up without an alarm. That helps a lot."

"That's a relief. I could fall asleep standing up today!"

Neena laughs and I feel the same rush I'd had running through the forest in my dream.

"I'm excited as well. I'm looking forward to learning how to create stuff and go into other people's dreams too," I add.

Neena smiles. "I'll teach you! I've been writing a guidebook for you in English but it's not finished yet. There's also the topic of jinn but let's go slow. You didn't see any more paris, did you?"

I shake my head. "Nope."

"OK. I'm so happy to have someone I can talk to about dreamweaving. In my hometown, we are still in touch with magic. I was worried that maybe ... maybe people here would think I am strange. My mum told me not to—"

Neena quickly stops herself and takes a breath. "Anyway, thanks for being my friend."

I feel a smile spread across my face at being called Neena's friend. "No one will think you're weird, I promise. Come on, let me properly introduce you to Tiffany and Murray – they'll love you!"

★

The next few days fly by in a blur. We spend every lunchtime together and Neena starts to come out of her shell with Tiff and Murray too. On Wednesday, Tiff says she'll introduce Neena to the drama club but when we get to the school hall no one is around.

"It's so strange, Tiffany," Mrs Williams the drama teacher says. "Everyone dropped out. They said they're not interested in acting any more."

Tiffany's shocked but we distract her by

playing with Murray's football in the playground. Ms Branberry even comes up to me and says well done for helping Neena settle in so well, which is a big relief.

But it's after school that the real work begins.

Every night Neena meets me in my dreams and teaches me how to dreamweave. She creates sprawling oak trees and fluorescent-pink flamingos just by concentrating and moving her hands. I try to copy her but the most I can manage is a tiny green shoot and a pink feather.

"It takes time," Neena keeps reassuring me. She says that I can control *anything* in my dream, even the weather, so I try to make it a sunny day on my clifftop. By the end of the week I can brighten the sky *ever so slightly* after *lots* of concentration. Neena congratulates me, saying it was a big achievement, but one night she dives off the cliff edge only to reappear,

flying
through
the air
with a
pair of huge
silver wings!
Now *that's* a big
achievement.

By night, I'm having these
amazing adventures but at school I can barely
keep my eyes open. Ms Branberry has caught
me dozing off more than once in class. It's a
small price to pay for actual real-life magic
but it does make things complicated.

★

On Friday we're sitting in geography when
Tiff pokes me in the arm. "Hey, sleepyhead,
Murray and I are having a sleepover at Eli's
house later. You coming?"

I glance over at Neena who quickly looks

down at her exercise book. A sleepover sounds fun but I need to keep dreamweaving. I still have so much to learn! How would I explain the symbol on my hand?

"Um, I think my parents want me home tonight, sorry," I say, feeling a bit guilty.

Murray looks at me and then to Neena. "Are you ditching us for her?"

Our teacher Mr Judd looks over and shushes Murray. I wait until he goes back to his marking.

"No, of course not," I snap back, not sure whether to be angry or sad.

Murray shrugs and goes back to his work while Tiff gives me and Neena a suspicious glare. I'll just have to make it up to them another time. Once I get the hang of dreamweaving I won't be so sleepy every day and things will go back to normal. But for now, I want to work on weaving a fluorescent-pink flamingo.

Harper Hopkins, who sits in front of me, shoots a hand up in the air. "Excuse me, sir. But could I be given an extra homework assignment today?" Harper says politely.

I'm a bit surprised since Harper usually spends most of the time doodling and cracking jokes. In fact, they can be a bit naughty and often get in trouble with the teachers. Mr Judd looks like his eyes might pop out of his head. "W-well, of course, Harper. But uh … wait, you aren't teasing me, are you?"

"Of course not. I want to make sure I catch up on the homework I missed last week," Harper says, a sweet smile on their face.

This is really weird.

"I've never seen Harper be interested in homework before," I whisper to Neena. "They're acting so … different."

Neena shrugs. "Maybe they just decided to

start trying harder. People change sometimes."

I nod, though something still feels off about the situation. Maybe it's just me feeling uneasy about change again, and a lot *has* changed recently. Harper Hopkins loving homework is nothing compared to finding out I'm a Dreamweaver.

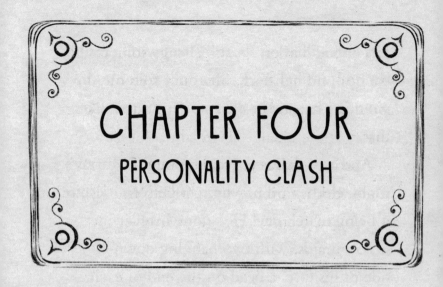

CHAPTER FOUR
PERSONALITY CLASH

The next day when I enter the classroom and see Murray and Tiffany sitting at our table, I immediately know something is off.

"What's Tiffany wearing?" Neena says, standing next to me in the doorway.

"I think it's P.E. kit," I say, horrified. The only physical activity Tiff does is dancing in school musicals.

But Tiff is sitting at our desk, her hair scraped back into a tight ponytail, rather than in her happy pigtail bunches. She isn't wearing her bright green glasses any more but instead has on sports glasses with a rubber band round her neck. She once told me she wouldn't be caught *dead* wearing a pair like that.

And as if that isn't weird enough, Murray's rugby clothes are nowhere to be seen, despite it being match day! He's done his hair in snazzy braids, with two hanging down either side of his face, a bead on the end of each. Not to mention the *silver puffer jacket* he's wearing, with the collar popped up. I mean, he looks really cool, but Murray has never cared about fashion before. And most of his clothes end up covered in mud from playing outside.

"Something isn't right," I whisper to Neena as we approach the desk. "Hi, guys, how are you?

Murray sticks one hand dramatically in the air and sings, "I'm doing just *fiiiiiiIIIIiiiIIInnee.*"

He holds the last note for ages, riffing up
and down very badly. Since when did Murray
sing?

"You sound like a cat on a roller coaster,"
Tiff says bluntly. "Now please shut it, I'm
trying to get into the zone for football."

"But Tiffany, you *love* singing," I gasp.
"And you *hate* physical exercise. Unless it's
a choreographed dance routine."

Tiffany rolls her eyes. "Phhst. Not any more. Singing and dancing is a waste of time. I'm focusing on football now."

Suddenly the penny drops. They're playing a trick on me!

"Aahhhhh, I get it, very funny, you two," I say sarcastically.

"What do you mean?" Murray says, head cocked to one side.

"I know you're upset I've been spending a lot of time with Neena but I've been trying to help her feel welcome here." I start to feel a bit hot in my cheeks. *Why should I have to apologize for that?*

"We like Neena," Tiff says and looks at me like *I'm* the one acting strange.

Maybe Tiff and Murray aren't pranking me. I turn to Neena who seems very concerned indeed.

"Tito, look," she says, pointing at the back of the class.

Leonard and Harry are squabbling *again*, their usually neat uniform unbuttoned and scruffy.

We hurry to an empty corner of the classroom away from the hubbub. "It's like everyone has changed personalities overnight!" I say.

"Overnight…" Neena whispered. "Or maybe we just haven't been paying attention. Didn't you say that people were acting weird last week as well?"

I get a sinking feeling in my stomach. "That's right! Like the drama club giving up acting, and Leonard and Harry fighting. Plus Harper Hopkins suddenly wanting more homework. I was having so much fun learning how to dreamweave I didn't notice how bad it was… And now Tiffany and Murray have swapped personalities. What do we do?"

"I don't know, they don't seem to realize

they've changed," Neena said, chewing on her lip. "I wouldn't normally suggest this, but if we went into Tiffany and Murray's dreams, we might be able to find out what's going on. The things people try to hide deep down often come out in dreams."

My mind immediately whirls back to earlier in the summer when I accidentally broke Roberto's favourite toy truck by dropping it in the bath. It got so wet that the lights stopped working and it didn't make a *vroom vroom* sound any more. I was too scared to tell my parents, so I hid it down the back of the sofa. But every night that week I had awful dreams about the truck coming to life and telling everyone what I did! They only stopped when I admitted what I'd done to Mama.

"They really do," I say with a shiver.

Neena starts rummaging in her backpack. "If we enter Tiffany and Murray's dreams, we might find out what's caused this!"

I look over my shoulder at my friends. They both look so *different*. Not that different is bad of course but … they don't look happy. Tiffany seems stressed, her brow wrinkled as she listens to music and "gets in the zone" for football (whatever that means). Murray is attempting to riff like an RnB singer, getting more and more frustrated when he can't hit the notes.

It's chaos. I have to find out what's going on. "I'm in."

"Great," Neena says, pulling something out of her backpack. It's a large notebook bound in cream cloth. "But there's a few things we need to go over first."

So, you're a Dreamweaver...

Welcome to an exclusive and magical community.

You probably have a lot of questions, but here are some basics to start us off.

Dreamweavers have their own special dream - like a home base. When you fall asleep with just your symbol on your hand you'll end up here first.

You can enter other people's dreams by creating a portal. They have to be asleep or the portal will not appear.

If someone wakes up while you're in their dream, you'll wake up too.

HOW TO DREAMWEAVE

Choose a symbol special to you. This will be the ticket into your own dream so keep it safe and only share it with those you trust!

Draw the symbol on your hand before you go to sleep.

When you finally fall asleep, you'll arrive in your

own special dream. You can now control it! With practice, you can make things appear - a monkey riding a bike, a human-sized doughnut ... anything's possible!

FYI

If you want to enter the dream of someone else who isn't a Dreamweaver, you must be holding a belonging of theirs when you fall asleep. In your dream, by focusing on that person, a portal will appear that takes you to their dream.

If you want to enter the dream of another Dreamweaver, you must know their symbol and draw it on your hand.

Warning!

Entering someone's dream without permission should only be done in extreme circumstances! Dreamweavers who use their powers for evil are called Darkweavers. You do not want to become one of them...

"Most of my journal is written in Khowar so I've translated some of it into English for you," Neena explains. "It's not complete yet but these are the most important things you need to know."

I run a finger across the page, which has an intricate border drawn around it. Something flutters in my chest, like a tiny butterfly. Neena has written this journal just for me... I feel like I'm part of a very special club.

I review the page of rules again and my eyes settle on the word Darkweaver, etched into the page in jet-black ink. Just the look of it sends shivers down my spine.

"Are there really people who use this gift for evil?" I ask quietly, not really wanting to hear the answer.

"Yes... But don't worry, Tito, it's very rare." Neena tries to sound casual but I notice her eyebrow twitch.

"Have you ever met one?" I ask.

Neena's back stiffens. "Let's focus on Tiffany and Murray. Do you understand that going into other people's dreams is only for extreme circumstances? It is a personal place."

I drop the topic of Darkweavers since Neena obviously doesn't want to talk about it. "I understand. We're only going into Tiffany and Murray's dream so we can find a way to help them."

"We need a belonging from each of them," Neena says, looking in their direction.

The school bell rings and Ms Branberry walks in to take registration. I pack away my dreamweaving journal safely in my bag and we go to join Murray and Tiff at our table.

"I'll collect the items," I say, figuring it will seem less weird if I get caught rummaging around in their bags.

"Thank you. It doesn't need to be anything

big," Neena whispers, as we get to our seats. "I will meet you in your dream tonight before we dreamhop into Tiffany and Murray's."

I'm struck by how weird that sounds. But then I see Murray fixing his hair in the reflection of a metal ruler, and Tiffany spinning a football on her finger. Everything has been strange since starting back at school.

Can Neena and I really put things back to normal?

★

I set my alarm clock for 7.30 a.m. and check it a few times before getting into bed. I haven't got the hang of waking myself up yet, and tonight's the first time I'll be in someone *else's* dream.

I've never thought so hard about what to wear to bed before. Should I put on my

fleece pyjamas in case Murray's dream is
in the Arctic? Or should I be hopping
into a pair of swimming trunks in case
Tiffany's dream is underwater? (I hope not.
I've only got my 25m swimming badge so
far.) I decide to ask Neena whether I can
change my outfit in my dream, that way all
bases are covered. Besides, a cape would be
cool in *any* circumstance.

I carefully take out Murray and Tiffany's
belongings from my bag. I managed to swipe
one of Murray's rugby socks from his P.E.
kit and a throat lozenge from Tiffany's bag.
They definitely weren't the *nicest* items but
I chose something they wouldn't notice was
missing. You know, I used to think of magic
as sparkles, fairy tales and Disney, not smelly
socks and sticky sweets!

I check that my symbol is drawn clearly
on my hand, then I lie back in bed, clutching
the strange items.

I don't know
how I'm
supposed to
go to sleep
holding
a stinky
sock,
though…
It feels
odd and
it's keeping
me from
drifting off.

I try to focus on something else to distract
me from the offensive smell. Something fun
– like maybe today's the day I finally change
the weather on my clifftop. If I just focus
really hard … and think about sunshine…

Rainbows…

A cool…

Breeze…

I open my eyes, blinking in the bright light. I've arrived on my clifftop but something's different…

"It's daytime!" I cheer, punching a hand in the air.

I've finally been able to change my dream!

"Tito, you brought the sun out!" I hear Neena's voice and turn round.

She's jumping through a portal by the pine trees, applauding me. I do an over-the-top bow.

"See! Your dreamweaving powers are getting stronger, it just takes practice," Neena says.

I blush but I do feel pretty good about finally being able to control my dream. In fact, why don't I try…

I close my eyes and bring an image up in my mind, keeping my breathing slow. A warm, shimmery feeling surrounds my body and when I open my eyes –

"Yay, I made a Dreamweaving outfit!"
I sing, spinning around.

"It looks a bit like mine!"

I'd imagined some baggy trousers in
the same style as Neena's with a T-shirt in
matching dark purple.

"We're a dreamweaving team, so I thought
we should match. Wait." I snap my fingers.
"We can be the Dream Team!"

"Perfect! I've never been part of a team
before..." Neena grins. "OK, teammate, let
me see Tiffany and Murray's items."

I reach into the pocket of my new baggy
trousers and pull out the sock and lozenge.

"This is what you chose?" she says, one
eyebrow raised.

"I didn't have much time!"

Neena absolutely cracks up, particularly at
the sock. Once she's calmed down, she picks
up the lozenge carefully with her thumb and
forefinger, like it might bite her.

"OK, they'll work. I'm guessing this is Tiffany's." Neena looks determined. "To enter her dream, we hold her item and concentrate all our thoughts on her. Then, if she is asleep, a portal will open that takes us to her dream."

A thought suddenly crosses my mind. "What if she isn't dreaming?"

Neena cocks her head to one side. "You *always* dream, even if you don't remember it when you wake up."

I try to think about how many sleeps I've had in my life (including the naps). I've definitely had some vivid dreams before, but I don't remember *all* of them. There must have been thousands! Maybe I've even been to my clifftop before and just not remembered it. It makes my brain start to hurt.

Neena is holding the lozenge and focusing straight ahead of her, so I focus too. After a few moments, the air in front of us starts going wobbly.

Then a spark of gold appears, fizzing and shooting out tiny stars like a sparkler. It grows in size, shining and stretching into a golden hoop with inky blackness inside.

"N-now what?" I stammer.

"We step through," Neena says simply.

I stare into the black void and my legs go weak. How can I step into that, not knowing where it leads? Me, the boy who can't even watch a slightly scary film at a sleepover?

"You can do it, Tito," Neena says softly.

I take a deep breath and think about my best friends giving up their lifelong dreams. And all the other kids in my class who have been acting strangely. I need to find out what's going on, whether it's scary or not.

"OK, I'm ready but you go first."

Neena nods and steps forwards. When she's halfway through, the rest of her gets sucked in quickly.

It totally freaks me out.

"I have to do this," I say, hopping up and down. "I can do this."

I close my eyes,

3, 2, 1!

I walk straight ahead – into the portal and into the unknown.

CHAPTER FIVE
DREAMHOPPING

I'm suspended inside the portal, surrounded by nothingness. I try not to panic but the sucking sensation is like nothing I've ever felt before. I hold my breath and just when I think I can't take it much longer, I feel gravity kick back in and my feet are on solid ground.

I'm taking a moment to wait for my legs to stop shaking, when Neena shouts in my ear. "Open your eyes!"

I yelp but do as she says. We're standing on a huge stage in a crowded arena in front of a cheering crowd! I realize why Neena had to shout to be heard.

"This seems like a normal Tiffany dream," I yell, over the hubbub. "Being onstage in front of an audience."

"But look over there!" Neena yells back, pointing to the crowd.

I follow her gaze and see huge, blow-up footballs with googly eyes being bounced around. The crowd is getting annoyed at the balls bonking them on the head and the cheers turn into boos. They even start throwing tomatoes at the stage. I have to duck quickly to avoid being splatted in the face!

Then, as I get my balance back, I see them.

The same glowing figures that were in my dream – and they are an angry neon red. They're circling Tiffany as she stands at a microphone trying to sing.

"Th-they were in my dream," I say,
backing away. "But they didn't look so …
scary."

"Those are paris," Neena replies, looking
pale. "And you're right. There is something
wrong. Do you remember the sketch I showed
you in my notebook?"

I think back to the sketch Neena had
shown me the first time we spoke in the
dining hall. She'd drawn spindly little figures

with cheeky grins. When I focus on the
figures circling Tiffany's head, I notice
their spiky hair and snarling faces.

Neena turns to me, her face grave.
"You know the beasts you read about
online, the ones from 'folklore'?"

I nod slowly, not liking where this is going.

"Well … they're actually real." Neena
searches my face for a reaction. "We call them
jinn – magical creatures that can sometimes

come into our dreams. I know I should have introduced them to you sooner but I wanted you to have fun dreamweaving first."

"Jinn…" I breathe deeply, keeping a fixed stare on the fairies.

We creep nearer to Tiffany so we can hear what the creatures are saying. It's horrible.

"You'll never be a star," they taunt in screeching voices. "You should give up!"

Tiffany is trying to bat the fairies away and continue singing but the crowd keep booing her.

"The crowd hates you. Give up singing and do something else. How about football?" one of the larger fairies snickers.

"But I hate sports!" Tiffany cries, getting more frustrated.

"No, you *love* football now. You need a personality change. People will like you more if you change!" the larger fairy says into her ear.

"Will they?" Tiffany asks, her eyes wide.

My fists are curled in rage and hot anger fills my chest. I can't take it any more! These horrible creatures are tormenting my best friend! Before I know it, I'm running forwards, waving my arms. "Enough! Leave her alone!"

At the sound of my voice, which I didn't know could be so loud, the fairies turn in shock. When they see me they whirl up into the sky and disappear through a shining portal.

"Quick, we must follow them!" Neena yells, grabbing my hand and running after the fairies.

"But the portal is so high, we'll never reach it," I babble, trying to keep up.

"It's a dream, we can do anything," Neena shouts back.

She grabs me around the waist, bends her knees and jumps! We soar up into the air, flying towards the portal. Shining silver wings fold out of Neena's shoulder blades and beat hard as we go higher and higher.

I close my eyes just before we hurtle through the portal and are sucked through into darkness.

A few seconds later we tumble out, landing in some prickly bushes. I groan and look down at my hands, which are covered in squelchy brown stuff.

"Ew, what is this?" I try to wipe it off on some cleaner grass.

"It's just mud," Neena laughs, as her wings fizzle into thin air behind her.

"When are you going to teach me to fly?" I say, and Neena's cheeks go a little pink.

"Honestly, I didn't even plan to dreamweave those, it just kind of happened."

We wipe off the mud as best we can and look around, trying to figure out where we are. We seem to be in a big field with overhead lights in the distance. We trek towards them and as we get closer, it becomes obvious that the field is a pitch of some kind.

"Look, it's Murray!" I point to a figure in the middle of the pitch. He's holding a rugby ball but the fairies are there, trying to prise it out of his hands.

"Sing for us! Sing for us!" the fairies chant.

"I have to stop them," I gasp, but Neena catches my hand and pulls me back.

"Wait. I know you want to help your friend. I do too. But if we go over there the paris will just run away again. We have to watch them and figure out what's going on. And if we startle Murray and he wakes up, we'll wake up too."

I nod reluctantly. I have to trust Neena on this stuff. I've only been dreamweaving for a week – she's had years of experience. Neena holds out a hand and her notebook materializes. It's the same one she showed me that contained the sketches.

"*This* is the Jinncyclopedia," she says, holding up the book.

"What did you just call your notebook?" I'm learning a lot of new vocab being friends with Neena.

"You'll see. My family passed it down to me and I've been making additions to it on my Dreamweaving adventures. Everything you need to know about jinn is in these pages."

The Jinncyclopedia

The world we live in isn't the only one. The human world and the spirit world exist side by side, separated by a realm in between. This is the realm we visit when we dream.

Humans and spirits, or jinn, exist in separate realms and neither can cross into the other.

But one place they can encounter each other is the in between. The dream realm.

The following pages of this encyclopedia contain descriptions of jinn that we have encountered and what we know about them.

Warning: Though most jinn are friendly, if a little mischievous, they should still be approached with caution. There is much we still don't know about these creatures.

I'm breathing quickly as my eyes scan the page. Spirits. Jinn. I start to feel dizzy and sit down on the grass, not caring about the mud any more.

Neena quickly bends down, worry all over her face. "Are you OK? I'm sorry, please don't be scared!" She sits down next to me, making a huge *squelch*.

Despite my fear and the wackiness of the situation, I start to laugh. A lot.

"I'm glad you still have your sense of humour." Neena grins. "And look, paris are usually good jinn. It says right here: 'Paris are playful tricksters who love nature, caring for flowers and trees. They often speak in riddles or rhyme and will only talk to you if you communicate with them similarly. They *love* sweet food, music and dancing. They take the form of multicoloured flying figures, small and human-shaped but with pretty wings.'"

I look at the illustration then squint back at the figures circling Murray.

"So why are they trying to convince the kids in our class to change their personality?" I say, shivering.

Neena looks very serious. "There's only one thing I can think of that would cause the paris to change their physical form and act like this. I think… I think they are under a spell."

I put my head in my hands.

As if this couldn't get any weirder.

★

The next day I had to go to the dentist so I missed the first class of school. Sitting in the dentist chair with my mouth wide open going "ahhhh" I couldn't help my mind from drifting back to the image of Murray and Tiffany's unhappy faces in their dreams. The fairies telling them to give up the things they loved and switching their identity overnight. It was like how they'd tried to convince me that I'm mean and nasty. As Mama says, I'm "*sensitivo*" and I *know* I'm not mean.

"Tito, mi amore, you are so quiet," Mama says. "Was it scary at the dentist?"

"No, I'm just tired."

I can't exactly tell Mama that scary fairies are tormenting my friends…

"How's it going with the new girl? Have you become friends?" Mama asks.

I'm shocked that I've forgotten to tell my parents. "Yes, we have. You were right, she was homesick. She's really nice actually."

"*Bravo*, Tito." Mama smiles. "I knew you would get through to her! You must invite her round for dinner, yes?"

For some reason the idea of Neena coming round for dinner seems weird. I guess because most of our friendship so far has involved magical adventures and supernatural creatures. I don't even know where Neena lives! She's mentioned her mum before … and her grandma too, I think. But now that I think about it, I don't really know that much about her. When I've tried to ask about her family, she doesn't want to share.

"I'll ask her," I reply to Mama. *About dinner, and other things too.*

We pull into the school car park. I kiss Mama goodbye and get a sticky hug from Roberto who's strapped in a car seat eating a lolly.

I don't like getting to school later than usual. There's no one around and even though Mama called to explain I was at the dentist, I still feel like I'm in trouble.

I hurry over to the front entrance of the school and walk into the reception. It's the middle of lesson time but the school is deserted. When I peek into the classroom windows I notice no one is inside.

Where is everybody?

Ms Julie the receptionist is sitting behind the desk looking exhausted. I go up to the counter to sign in. "Good morning, Ms Julie. I'm signing in late from the dentist."

"Ahh, it's been a hectic morning, Tito," she says, rubbing her eyes. "I don't know what's got into the students but they've *all* been acting up. Maybe they're excited for the weekend…"

My stomach drops. Acting up?

"At least you seem your normal sensible self." She smiles. "You'll have to join everyone in the hall. The whole school is in there."

A horrible sense of dread washes over me. I walk down the empty corridor towards the school hall where I can hear a rumble of voices. As I get closer a boy in Year Six bursts through the doors laughing, and starts running down the corridor, followed by our P.E. teacher!

"Jeffrey, get back here!"

I step back as they run past, aware of the noisy ruckus coming from the school hall. I can vaguely make out our head teacher Mr Tulley's voice shouting over the hubbub but I can't really hear what he's saying. When I creep inside the hall my jaw drops at what I see.

The whole school is crammed in there, sitting around in messy lines. Well, half of them are sitting, the other half are up causing what my mum would call "pandemonium". There are students climbing the exercise ropes pinned back to the wall. A group in the corner appear to be having a water fight with their bottles. I see at least four arguments, two dance battles and one year group that look like they're doing yoga. *Everyone* is acting strangely, whether loud and rowdy or anxious and fretting.

And the teachers don't have a *clue* what to do.

I spy Ms Branberry at the front of our class group, holding Leonard and Harry apart as they go at it again in another flappy hand fight. The other teachers are either in among the crowd, trying to break up arguments, or standing at the top of the hall looking shocked.

I carefully weave my way through the chaos to where my class are sitting and hear Mr Tulley's voice, this time coming through a megaphone.

"Everybody, settle down. NOW!!!!!"

It works … a bit. The room settles slightly. I spot Neena, sitting in between Football Tiff and Pop Star Murray. They seem to be bickering and Neena is trying to calm them down. As soon as Neena spots me, she looks relieved.

"What's happening?" I ask.

"Everyone's switched personalities. It's a mess," she says. "And Tiffany and

Murray keep arguing."

"About what?" I've never heard my friends argue about *anything* before. They sometimes tease each other but never seriously.

Tiffany overhears me and turns round, her face sour. "Murray keeps humming and dancing around. It's *sooooo* annoying." She shoots Murray a hard stare over my shoulder. "I cannot believe I was ever friends with him."

Murray immediately leans forwards and starts singing loudly. "*Mmmmmm la la laaaaa, you're just jealous because I'm so good at singing!*" he belts, extremely off-key.

Tiffany grabs her football and attempts to throw it at Murray but accidentally hits me in the face instead.

"Ow!" I yelp, rubbing my nose.

"Your head was in my way," Tiff says bluntly.

"Tiffany, Murray, you two are friends,

remember?" Neena pleads. "Best friends."

But Tiffany just turns back round in a huff.

"I could never be friends with someone who doesn't appreciate the arts," Murray snaps and turns up the collar of his snazzy jacket to hide his face.

Things are getting worse by the second.

"Listen up, everyone," Mr Tulley announces. "If this is a practical joke, it ends now! You will be missing your lunch break until this stops!"

The school hall immediately erupts into

shouts of "that's not fair" and Mr Tulley's face goes bright red.

"This isn't going to end unless we do something," Neena says to me, her voice urgent. "The paris are working quicker than we thought."

"And what if they get to us?" I shiver, remembering how they had taunted me in my dream.

Neena shakes her head. "They can't. Dreamweavers know when we're dreaming so their tricks don't work. But the rest of the school are vulnerable."

"You said they're normally good jinn," I say. "Do you really think someone could have put a spell on them?"

Neena looks as if she's thinking deeply, then she shakes herself and shrugs. "I'm not sure."

I get the niggling feeling *again* that she isn't telling me the full story. But I do know that Neena's right – we're the only ones that can do something. I feel a burning determination inside to help my friends. If I can dreamweave then I should use the gift to do something good. Even if my stomach is filled with butterflies at the thought of seeing the paris again.

"We should dreamhop again tonight," I say, pushing the fear aside. "Try to find the scary fairies."

I spot Leonard's head-of-year badge, hanging loosely from his school bag as he picks a fight with a boy in the next class. I reach out and unhook it, slipping it into my pocket. I'll return it tomorrow – it's not like Leonard is acting much like the Head of Year anyway!

Neena watches me and nods. "If the paris are under a spell, we'll have to find a way to remove it. I'll do some reading tonight from one of my family's dreamweaving journals to see if there's anything that can help."

I seize the opportunity to ask Neena a question. "So some of your family are Dreamweavers too? Maybe they can help us!"

"No, they can't," Neena snaps. "We can do this by ourselves."

"But surely they can—"

My question is cut off by Mr Tulley. "You will be silent NOW or you'll be staying after school!"

Reluctantly the room quietens down. Apparently, the threat of after-school detention is the only thing that can calm the chaos.

I sigh and feel a slight heat in my cheeks from Neena snapping at me. Why won't she tell me about her family? She's even turned to face away from me now, so she can avoid my eyeline.

I'll try again later when we go into Leonard's dream – where we'll face the scary fairies once again.

CHAPTER SIX
NIGHTMARE

At 9 p.m. sharp I announce I'm going to bed.

"You're being very punctual with your bedtimes recently," Mum says, half watching the TV.

"He is a big boy now," Mama says, reading a book in the big armchair. "He makes his own schedule."

"Well, well. We'll have to start calling you Mr Tito soon, eh?" Mum winks.

I roll my eyes and laugh. "Please don't, Mum. Goodnight."

"Buona notte, darling," Mama says,

blowing a kiss. "Please check on Roberto before you go to sleep?"

I nod my head and blow a kiss back to them before heading up our squeaky staircase, avoiding the wobbly step. I poke my head around Roberto's open door. Berto is sleeping soundly in his cot, the yellow glow of his night light making the room feel cosy and warm. When he's asleep he's very cute. I wonder what he dreams about... I hope he has nice dreams, safe from jinn and scary fairies. Maybe when he's older he'll be a Dreamweaver too. It might run in families. I smile at the thought of teaching Berto how to weave giant jam doughnuts or rainbow-coloured racing cars.

I leave his room and tiptoe across the landing to mine, thinking of all the unanswered questions I still have about dreamweaving. Whenever I ask Neena she changes the subject. But now there's a real risk involved. Sure, the fairies seem to have only targeted the kids in our school so far (I wonder why that is...), but what if they started spreading to other people's dreams? I think of my baby brother being tormented by scary fairies and my tummy instantly clenches. For the first time, I realize I'm actually annoyed at Neena for keeping things from me.

But there's no more time to sit around wondering. We have to work quickly to stop the fairies before they spread their evil any further. I want my friends back.

As I retrace my symbol on my hand in biro, I notice the time. It's already 9.15 p.m. and I'd agreed to meet Neena at 9.30 p.m. in my dream. I quickly set the alarm, get into bed and clutch Leonard's head-of-year badge in my hand.

I close my eyes, squirm around until I feel comfy and then…

Sssslowly, I driffft…

Offf…

Almost as soon as I arrive in my clifftop dream, a golden portal opens and Neena steps out. The fogginess and confusion I used to feel when I arrived in my dream has gone. I know exactly where I am and why. I think my powers are getting stronger.

"Tito, hi!" Neena says, walking up to me in her Dreamweaver outfit. I quickly weave mine around me too, adding a pocket to hold Leonard's head-of-year badge.

"Sorry I'm a bit late. Maybe I should meet you in your dream next time?" I say.

Neena's eyes flicker. "That's OK. Did you bring the badge?"

"It's in my pocket," I say, trying to brush

away the irritation I feel growing inside my chest at Neena dodging my questions. "What's the plan?"

"I'm going to try to talk to the paris," says Neena. "I've met their kind before so I know how they speak. Remember what it said in the Jinncyclopedia? They like riddles and rhymes. Maybe I can find out whether they are under a spell and where it came from."

"And why they've come here," I add. "Don't you wonder why they've only targeted our school?"

Neena shivers. "Mmhmm."

I'm not so sure about this plan. I mean, the fairies just ran away from us before. But Neena does know more about jinn than me so I take a deep breath and gather all the courage I have.

"Do you want to try to open the portal to Leonard's dream?" Neena offers. "You're becoming more powerful. I know you can do it."

"Oh … yes. I do feel stronger." I smile, the excitement creeping in. "How do I do it?"

Neena comes to stand by my side. She takes a wide stance and holds her hands in front of her, palms up. I copy her, feeling a little foolish but trying to pretend I look in control and not like a toddler doing karate.

"Now focus on the object and bring an image of Leonard to your mind. Clear your thoughts of anything else," Neena instructs, her voice calm and even.

I close my eyes and focus on the head-of-year badge in my pocket. I can just feel the metal corner poking into my thigh, which helps. Then I bring up an image of quiet, well-behaved and sensible Leonard in my mind.

"Tito, open your eyes," whispers Neena.

I open one eye and see a golden spark in front of me, growing larger and larger, sputtering out little gold stars as it grows.

"I–I did it!" I stammer. "I opened the portal!"

Neena actually jumps up and down, clapping her hands together.

I join her jumping up and down, completely taken over by the thrill of making *actual magic* happen.

"OK," I say finally, catching my breath. "Let's find those fairies and save our friends."

Neena gestures for me to go first, so I lift

my head high and walk towards it, trying to stop my legs from shaking. It is *my* portal, after all.

I feel the inky substance engulf my body for a few seconds. I'll never get used to that. Then I'm quickly sucked through to the other side. I wait a few seconds for my eyes to adjust to the bright light on the other side of the portal and then realize where I am. This dream is in my classroom at school but with a few BIG changes.

"Oh no!" Neena gasps, coming through the portal behind me.

The room is completely wrecked! Desks and chairs have been pushed over and graffiti is sprayed on the walls. There's rubbish and clutter strewn all over the floor and written on the whiteboard in big letters is:

SCHOOL SUCKS!

I look out of the window that overlooks the playground and finally locate Leonard.

He is terrified. The fairies have trapped him inside the climbing frame and are throwing crayons and pencils at him!

"The fairies are out there with Leonard. Do you really think they'll listen to you?" I ask, not convinced.

"We'll stay in here and talk to them through the window, and maybe they'll be less spooked," Neena says. "I'll talk to them in rhyme. We just need to keep their attention long enough to find out what happened to them."

Neena unlocks the classroom window and slowly slides it open. With each creak of the glass I'm certain the fairies will bolt. I hold my breath until finally the window is fully open. Neena takes a deep breath and begins.

"Paris, paris, what happened here?

You were never bringers of fear!"

The red-eyed fairies whip their tiny heads round and stare at us menacingly. They reply as one, in a shrill tone,

"Being evil is much more fun,
Name yourself, little one."

Neena takes a breath, unsure what to do.
Then she puffs her chest and replies,

"Neena Ahlaam. Now you tell,
Is this evil from a spell?"

The paris start circling Leonard again,
getting faster, and it seems like they aren't
going to answer. I watch them flying, round
and round, then suddenly I hear myself
shouting:

"Why torment our school so?
Tell us, fairies, what you know!"

Neena tenses up, like she's afraid we might
have pushed them too far, but the scary
fairies finally answer:

"A spell, yes, a spell, it's true,
But we were sent to locate *you*."

A chill runs down my spine. They're
looking straight at Neena.

"The fairies were sent to find you?" I whisper to Neena, too terrified to speak any louder. "By who?"

But Neena simply stares out of the window, trembling. She seems frozen to the spot, not even blinking.

"Neena? Neena, are you OK?" I ask, shaking her gently. But Neena looks back at me blankly, tears forming in her eyes.

I watch helplessly as the fairies fly off towards the edge of the playground where the trees begin. They seem to be doing some kind of dance, throwing their hands in the air and making a beckoning motion at the same time.

Then I notice something. One of the fairies has drifted away from the pack towards a snowdrop, which is pushing up through the grass by an old oak tree. I lean forwards and see the fairy has landed on the flower.

"Look, Neena," I say, jostling her. "That fairy's acting different from the others."

Neena's face turns from shock to amazement as she watches the stray fairy. As it relaxes on the flower its eyes stop glowing red and its spiky hair falls into flowing waves.

"It looks like the spell's wearing off. The flower is reminding the pari of its true purpose – to care for nature." Neena wipes the tears from her eyes. "M-maybe we *can* break the spell."

Another fairy notices the flower and is drawn to it, like a bee to a rose. The two fairies start frolicking around the flower together, their colour changing to a silver sheen and their eyes turning big and bright.

"I think this is going to work," I say, bouncing on the spot. "The fairies are going to break the spell, we just need the rest to go to the flower."

But at that moment, a horrible neon-green light blasts out from the sky, above where the other fairies are dancing. It spreads and expands into a swirling portal, larger than any I've seen before.

Sweat breaks out on my forehead and I feel Neena reach for my hand as a horrifying sight appears.

One long, thin leg stretches out of the portal.

Then another leg appears and an arm, before the towering figure is in the playground, staring into the distance with piercing green eyes.

I know instantly who this man is.

A Darkweaver.

Neena tugs me down to the ground so we'll be hidden, but something tells me I need to see this. Some of my questions might finally be answered. I carefully peek up through the window to watch.

The man is holding his hands out in front of him, emitting wobbly green waves. When the waves hit the fairies on the snowdrop, their eyes immediately glow red once more and their scary fairy appearance returns.

"Well… Where is she?" he purrs in a sinister, silky voice.

The man looks around and I duck quickly as his eyes pass over the window. *Please say he didn't see me*, I pray. My mouth has gone completely dry.

After waiting a few more agonizing moments, I gather all my courage and slowly peer through the window.

The man strides to the middle of the playground, almost as if he's gliding. Then he stands and closes his eyes.

"I do not sense her here," he growls, looking at the fairies angrily. "Do you have any idea how much power it takes for me to travel here?"

The fairies shrink away from him and cower in a group. I *almost* feel sorry for them.

"I will inform the alliance of your findings," he says slowly. Then he steps back through his portal, followed reluctantly by the fairies, leaving nothing behind.

I crouch in fear for a moment longer, not sure that my body can be unfrozen from this position.

"Who ... was ... he?" I ask, breathless with terror.

But Neena doesn't reply.

I turn to where Neena had been beside me, but there's no one there.

Then I see it, the tiniest speck of gold as a portal closes on the other side of the classroom.

"Neena!" I call, panic rising in my chest.

But the portal has closed. She's left me, alone in a strange dream. With a possible Darkweaver on the loose.

I suddenly feel like the classroom is getting smaller and smaller. The lights begin to flicker and darkness clouds the windows.

"Calm down, Tito," I say to myself, my voice shaking. The more frightened I feel, the scarier the dream gets. Cracks begin to appear up the walls of the classroom and horrible howls echo through the open window. I'm dreamweaving myself into a nightmare!

I think of poor Leonard outside but I'm too scared to move from my position. I hug my knees close to my chest and feel my heart beating hard.

How could she just leave me here?

I try to wake myself up, closing my eyes

tight and then
opening them
quickly. But
no matter
how hard
I try, I'm
still in the
classroom.

"Wake
up! Wake up!"
I scream. But
nothing happens.

*Maybe I can make
a portal back to my own dream.* I hold my
hands out but they are shaking, and I can't
concentrate enough to make the portal
appear.

My only hope now is to wait for my alarm
to go off and wake me up. Or for Leonard
to wake up and kick me back out into the
waking world. But how long will that take?

And will the Darkweaver come back before
then?
   With shadows moving across the walls
and scuttling noises coming from the hallway,
I sit in terror.
   And wait.

Nightmares

For centuries, artists, writers, philosophers and spiritual leaders have come up with theories about nightmares. What do they mean? Where do they come from? And what causes them?

Dreamweavers know the truth. Nightmares are not separate to dreams. They are simply the dark side of the dreaming mind. Any dream can turn dark when fear, anger or sadness take over.

But nightmares are misunderstood. Just as we need to know rain to enjoy the sun, all dreamers must experience dark dreams and light. Sometimes nightmares have a lesson to teach us.

Although Dreamweavers enjoy exploring the fun and adventurous parts of our dreams, we shouldn't be afraid of exploring those darker and forgotten corners. You may just find the answers you seek.

CHAPTER SEVEN
THE TRUTH WILL PROTECT YOU

"Knock, knock! Wake up, lazybones."

I roll over in bed and open my bleary eyes. Mum is standing in the doorway. My alarm had *finally* gone off at 8 a.m. but I couldn't get out of bed. Thank goodness it was Saturday! Even when Rupert came bounding up the stairs, I stayed wrapped up in my duvet cocoon. Rupert settled down at the foot of my bed, resting his soft chin on my legs. I think he was comforting me.

"I don't feel like getting up, Mum," I say in a small voice.

"What's wrong?" Mum comes and crouches down next to my bed, her face close to mine.

"I don't know… Maybe I'm poorly," I lie, not able to tell her the truth – that my new friend abandoned me in a nightmare.

"Poorly?" comes a worried voice on the other side of the door. Mama appears, Roberto balanced on her hip. "You need my chicken zuppa, baby? I'll make a big batch for my sensitivo boy."

Mum smiles and winks at me. "I think Tito just needs a little bit more of a lie-in this morning, don't you?"

Before I can answer, the phone rings and Mama goes out to answer, Roberto bouncing in her arms.

"When you feel like it, come down to the shed and we can make hot chocolate." Mum ruffles my hair and walks out. Sometimes I get annoyed when my parents make a fuss of me but right now I'm grateful for the comfort. Rupert lets out a big sigh, like he feels a bit better too.

I lie still for a little while longer. Just as I'm considering rolling out of bed, Mama appears again at the door, holding the phone out to me.

"Carino, it's for you." She tosses me the phone. "It's Neena. She seems very nice."

Of course Mama spoke to her for five minutes before coming up! I take the phone and Mama leaves me to talk to Neena. Although after what she did, I don't really want to speak to her.

"Hi, Tito, I got your number from the school directory. I hope you don't mind," Neena says quietly.

I don't reply. Hearing her voice reminds me of how hurt I feel.

"Your mama seems really nice." Neena keeps talking to fill the silence. "She played me an opera song over the phone."

"Yeah, she does that," I reply quietly. Then, with Rupert's reassuring head resting on my legs, I feel a surge of confidence. "What happened, Neena? You left me all alone. I was so scared that the dream turned into a nightmare! I couldn't wake up and I couldn't leave the dream so I just had to wait there. You abandoned me!"

There's a moment of silence while Neena searches for the right words to say. "I'm so sorry. I thought you would have left through a portal like I did. That's why I'm ringing – to say sorry. I shouldn't have left like that. I know you're new to this. I'm so sorry the dream turned dark."

I still feel hurt but hearing Neena apologize helps. And now that I've opened up about how I feel, I want to keep going.

"Who was that man?" I say, the words tumbling out. "There are so many things about dreamweaving, about your past, that I don't know. If we have any chance of stopping the scary fairies and changing my friends back to normal, you have to be honest with me. I thought we were a team."

There's another pause and Neena sighs heavily. "You're right, Tito. You deserve the full story. Can you meet me at the park by the school? I'll tell you everything in person."

"I'll ask my mama to take me there in an hour," I say, with a firmness in my voice that

I haven't heard before.

"Oh, and Tito," Neena quickly adds. "We *are* a team, if you can trust me again."

I can hear she means it. But she has some explaining to do first.

★

Mama agrees to take me to the park since Roberto "needs some fresh air". He's been hyper all morning and sprinting around the living room, so I think she is actually trying to tire him out.

When we get there Neena is waiting in the middle of the grassy area. I convince Mama to stay in the baby play area with Berto while we speak.

"But you *have* to let me come and say hi after," she says, wagging a finger.

"I promise, Mama," I say, then squelch my way over the damp grass to where Neena is waiting.

Rupert runs ahead of me and Neena kneels down to greet him. He gives her a few doggy kisses and she laughs, stroking his head and letting him chew on her laces.

"Thank you for coming, I want to explain everything." Neena watches as Rupert runs off to sniff around in the mud.

I put my hands in my pockets then we start walking together, following Rupert's trail.

"We moved here two months ago. My mum, my grandma and me," Neena begins. "We live at the end of the row of houses opposite the school. All three of us are Soothsayers."

"Soupsayers?" I ask, surprised.

"*Sooth*sayers!" Neena repeats seriously
but I see the corners of her mouth twitch
into a smile. "I think that's the English word.
I looked it up in the dictionary."

"I'm sure it is, you're just teaching me a
lot of new words," I say. "So it doesn't mean
someone who can speak to soup?"

Neena giggles. "No! It's someone who is
in touch with the spirit realm. Lots of people
think it means you can see the future but
that is just one kind of Soothsayer. We can
be Dreamweavers, Healers, Fortune Tellers,
Psychics… And we are found all over the
Earth."

I suddenly feel like I'm seeing the world
for the first time. I look at the little rows of
houses that frame the park and imagine the
people who live inside. Were some of them
Soothsayers too?

"It's a lot to take in, I know. I wanted

to try to introduce you to things slowly,"
Neena says, looking at my shocked
expression. "But there's more and this
is the really important part."

Neena stops walking so I turn to face her,
ready to hear the full story – finally.

"My family didn't move here for work.
We were running away. The man that crashed
Leonard's dream last night, the Darkweaver…"
Neena takes a big breath. "That's my uncle
Rahim."

Rupert runs up with a big stick and thrusts
it into my hand. This is *so* not the time for
fetch! I throw the stick, which is tricky when
it feels like the world is spinning.

"That was your uncle? He's a
Darkweaver?" I whisper.

Neena has tears in her eyes as she carries
on. "Yes. He was an extremely talented and
powerful Dreamweaver. He taught me how
to dreamweave, and the Jinncyclopedia used

to belong to him before he gave it to me. But the power went to his head. He started talking about all these plans – to control the jinn and merge the spirit world with the human world. We tried to change his mind but it was too late… He disappeared. The Soothsayers in my hometown call him the Bhoot, which means the ghost. They were convinced I would follow in his footsteps. That I would become a Darkweaver too! The rumours got so bad that we decided to leave behind everything we knew. To get away from the town but also to hide from the Bhoot."

Neena is crying a lot now so I put my arm round her. Rupert even comes and sits on her feet.

"Don't worry, Neena, I know you won't become a Darkweaver." I try to sound reassuring. "But how did your uncle find you?"

Neena shakes her head. "I don't know. Someone must have told him we'd gone to the UK. Then he sent the paris to act as his scouts. He must have known that if they caused enough mayhem I'd go after them to try to put things right. Luckily I changed my symbol before I came. As long as he doesn't know yours or mine, our dreams are safe."

"You mean I can change my symbol to something cooler?"

Neena chuckles lightly but there's sadness in her eyes.

I refocus and try to piece together all this new information in my mind. "So are you telling me he's here? He entered Leonard's dream after all."

Neena looks pale as she considers this. "If he was in the UK, he'd just come and get me. He must still be in Pakistan, and there's a reason for him staying there."

I think back to what I heard the Bhoot

say last night. Neena might not have heard it before she left. I wrack my brains trying to remember his exact words.

"Your unc— I mean, the Bhoot. He said something to the fairies about it taking a lot of power for him to come here. Then he said something else … something about an alliance? Ugh, I can't remember."

Neena's eyebrows dart up. "An alliance? He said that?"

I nod, feeling more certain of what I heard.

"Then he *is* working with other Darkweavers. It takes a lot of power to cast a spell on jinn and even more to dreamweave remotely." Neena shudders and I know it isn't from the cold. "His plan to merge the spirit world and human world is under way. We *have* to save those paris and turn the school back to normal. I *have* to prove I'll only use my powers for good."

I reach out and take Neena's hand.

"I'm going to help you. After all, we are the Dream Team."

Neena smiles and Rupert leaps up. I think he wants to be part of the team too.

"Thank you. I'm sorry I didn't tell you the truth earlier, I just… I don't have many friends here and I thought if you knew who my uncle was, you wouldn't like me. I'm glad to finally have a teammate. And now I think it's about time I shared this with you." Neena holds up her hand to me. I let out a little excited squeak when I see what *her* symbol is.

"The smiling face with sunglasses!"

"I guess we were both inspired by emojis." Neena laughs.

I feel so pleased

that Neena trusts me enough with her symbol, and her dream. I don't want to change my symbol any more!

I hear Mama calling to me from the other side of the park. "I have to go back… Oh, and my mama wants to meet you," I add, feeling just a *bit* embarrassed.

"Of course. I'll tell you the plan to break the spell on the way." Neena puts her hands on her hips.

"There's a plan?" I ask.

"Oh yes," she replies, grinning at me. "There's always a plan."

CHAPTER EIGHT
PHASE ONE: FAIRY BAIT

The plan seems simple enough. We lure all the fairies into one dream where Neena will weave *loads* of flowers. Hopefully being in nature will remind the scary fairies of their true selves, breaking the spell. Then they'll stop bullying my friends (and the rest of the school) and they'll all go back to normal.

It's a straightforward plan.

It's a solid plan.

It's going to work… Right?

I've been going over it in my mind so many times that I don't even notice Mum has been calling my name.

"Earth to Tito... Hello?" she's saying, clicking her fingers over the dinner table.

I snap back to reality, shaking my head. "Huh?" There's a twirl of spaghetti on my fork that's been hanging in mid-air for so long now it's gone cold.

"Mama was just saying how nice it was to meet Neena," Mum says. "What's going on in that brain of yours?"

I shrug and eat my spaghetti. "Nothing."

"Well, I'm glad you are making new amici," Mama says, cutting up Roberto's chicken for him. "But I miss Tiffany and Murray. You haven't mentioned them since going back to school. How are they?"

I feel my stomach lurch and tears almost spring to my eyes. I didn't realize how much I missed my friends. It makes me feel even guiltier for not spending much time with them since Neena and I became friends.

But there has been so much going on!

"Tiff and Murray are fine," I lie.

They will be fine. I'm going to make sure of it.

When it's time for bed, I bring Rupert up with me. Something about having him there makes me feel calmer.

"If things get bad, wake me up, OK?" I say.

Rupert licks his bum in response. Some help he's going to be.

I set my alarm, check it three times and then draw Neena's symbol on my hand. For what I hope will be the last time, I grab Murray and Tiffany's items from the drawer and finally get into bed.

I have to stop Rupert from trying to eat the throat lozenge but once he settles down, I close my eyes and try to go to sleep. My whole body feels like it's buzzing with nerves and I can't seem to get comfy. I get an itch on my nose, then on my foot, then my pillow feels too hot and I have to turn it over.

Mama once taught me a technique to help me fall asleep so I give that a go.

I take five deep breaths, in and out.

Then I imagine myself in the mountains on a fresh, sunny day. With each step I take up the mountain I count, first up to twenty then back down again.

Fifteen,

    Sixteen,

        Seven … teen…

            Eighteeeeeeeen…

        Nineeeeteen…

              Twennnnnnty…

                  …

I emerge on my clifftop and get straight to work. Focusing on Murray's rugby sock I hold my hands out to open a portal.

"Come on, come on…"

I grit my teeth and after a few seconds

of horrible nothingness, tiny sparks appear.
Then a golden portal slowly grows and
I waste no time in jumping straight through.

I'm spat out the other side on to the
rugby pitch in Murray's dream. It's lit up by
floodlights but the rain is so heavy that it's
hard to make out where anyone is. I close
my eyes and weave a large hood on to my
dreamweaving outfit, to keep the rain off my
face. Squinting, I scan the pitch through the
pelting rain for Neena.

But she isn't here.

My heart starts to beat a little harder before
I realize — we never agreed whose dream to
enter first! After all our discussion and going
over the plan a million times, we forgot the
first step!

A bolt of lightning rips through the sky
and I jump on the spot, goose pimples
running up my arms and neck. I really don't
want to be alone. Not again. I hear a voice

behind me and I turn to see Pop Star Murray
in the distance. The fairies look like they're
back, forcing him to sing into a stupidly tall
microphone. I want to run to him but my
feet won't move – it's like they're stuck in
the mud. I need Neena. I need to help my
friends!

"Neena!" I call out.

My voice rings around the pitch. It's loud enough to catch Murray's attention. I notice him turn in my direction, so I pull my hood further over my head. Even if Murray thinks this is just a dream, I don't want to be seen snooping about.

"Tito?" comes a voice in reply, like an echo at the back of a cave.

It's Neena.

"Neena!" I shout. "Where are you?"

I'm baffled as to how Neena heard me, but more than anything, I'm relieved.

"I'm in my dream! I thought you were coming here?"

"What? I thought we were meeting in Murray's dream?" I call. This situation is so ridiculous that I feel my fear disappearing.

"Noooo, you come here!" Neena calls back.

"No, you come here!" I'm smiling now.

There's a moment of silence. "Fine, I'm

coming. Wait there!"

I roll my eyes – like I have any other choice!

A minute later a golden portal appears a little way off to my right. Neena steps through holding Murray's other smelly P.E. sock.

"Lucky that I swiped this on Friday, huh?" Neena says, tucking the sock into the pocket of her baggy trousers. "Your dreamweaving skills get stronger every day! Speaking across dreams is hard but I heard you loud and clear."

I feel my cheeks blush at the compliment. "I just knew I *really* wanted to talk to you."

"Remember what I said? Only people who feel their emotions very strongly can be Dreamweavers. That *and* a huge imagination to be able to weave the most fantastic things. Like this…"

Neena holds out a hand in the rain and

the wiggly airwaves appear above it. Out of nowhere, a plate appears and is filled, one by one, with cream finger buns! The pastries pop into existence in a puff of icing sugar.

"This is our pari bait!" Neena announces. "All jinn love human food but paris especially love sweets. I saw these at the supermarket when I went with my mum and thought they would be perfect. Now let's stop this rain. No one likes soggy buns."

Neena clicks her fingers and in an instant, the skies above us clear into a starlit night. I feel my jaw hanging open at how easily Neena can dreamweave.

"What?" Neena says, seemingly unaware of her power. "Let's lure these paris into my dream!"

Without any warning, Neena sets off, running at breakneck speed towards Pop Star Murray and the paris. I quickly race after her, willing my legs to run faster to keep up.

There's a floaty feeling surrounding my feet and suddenly I'm sprinting faster than I ever could in real life! I never knew I could dreamweave myself to run quicker!

We finally reach the paris and a *very* startled-looking Murray. Neena holds the plate high above her head.

"What do humans have ten of, are soft in the middle and sweet to taste?" Neena says in a riddle.

The paris look up, eyes blazing red, and catch sight of the cream finger buns.

"Foooooooooooooooood!" they screech and start flying right at us!

"Run!" Neena bellows.

We set off together, running across the field so fast our legs are a blur. I sneak a look over my shoulder and see the fairies chasing behind us, reaching their spindly arms out and snatching at the air.

"Argh, don't look back!" I yelp.

We race across the endless rugby pitch as portals open and more fairies pour out.

"They're coming from everyone else's dreams. It's working!" Neena pants as she runs. "Keep going."

A portal opens directly in front of us and we have to skid to the right, narrowly avoiding running straight into it.

There are *so* many paris – they must have been all over the country searching

until they narrowed it down to our school.
The thought makes me shiver but I keep
running faster and faster. I feel like I'm flying!

I look down and stifle a scream. I *am*
flying! I'm only about fifteen centimetres
off the ground but speeding along without
my feet touching the grass. If it weren't for
the snapping fairies behind me, this would
actually be super fun!

"There are hundreds of them," I exclaim

as more portals open around us.

"Good! We need to get all of them. Let's lure them into my dream and trap them," Neena pants, holding on to the plate tightly with both hands while her legs paddle away at the speed of light underneath her.

Neena opens a sparkling gold portal in front of us, stretching it wide until it's the size of a swimming pool. Big enough that the fairies can't avoid it.

"Let's go!" she screams, diving head first into the portal.

Without turning to see the scary mob behind me, I follow – tumbling full speed into Neena's dream for the very first time.

CHAPTER NINE
PHASE TWO: PASTRY POWER

As soon as we fly into Neena's dream,
I see her weaving the next part of the plan.
Golden sparkling threads are shooting out of
her upturned hands and into the air. I watch
in amazement as the threads intertwine to
form a huge net. It hangs off the branch of a
tall, skinny tree in the small, leafy enclosure
we stand in.

She finishes it just in the nick of time,
and the fairies come crashing through the
portal into the newly formed net. Neena
closes it up quickly and the fairies thrash

about angrily inside.

I'm so transfixed by the sight that I almost forget where I am. I'm finally in Neena's dream!

I look out at the view beyond the tree-lined enclosure and gasp in awe. White chalk hills roll into a valley below where a sparkling river flows. A village of houses sits on the side of the valley, underneath a misty grey sky. It's beautiful, like a mystical town from a fairy tale.

"We're somewhere in Chitral, aren't we?" I say, looking out. "Your home."

Neena stands beside me, gazing at the view, her green eyes sparkling. "I miss it every day, but at least I can see it in my dreams. And I like my new home in the UK too … and my new friends."

She smiles sheepishly at me before clearing her throat. "Now, we better get back to business."

She turns to look at the bulging net full
of angry paris and addresses them in rhyme:
  "Paris of yellow, pink and blue,
  Remember your nature true,
  Tricksters yes, but monsters? No!
  Banish the spell that makes you so."
The fairies snarl and spit against the golden
net, their bodies red and twisted. Neena
repeats the rhyme again, louder and more
passionately but it makes no difference.
It's like the fairies can't hear her at all.

  "The spell is too strong," I despair.
"But I don't think they *want* to be evil.
They seem upset."

  "I don't think flowers or cream fingers
are enough to break the spell," Neena frets.
"What has my uncle *done*?"

  Neena slumps to the ground, her head in
her hands. The sky above us starts to cloud
and I know I have to do something quick
to take control of the situation.

I crouch down next to Neena and put a comforting hand on her shoulder. It's then that I notice something. A tiny, delicate white flower in the grass near where she is sitting. It's small, but enough to plant an idea in my mind.

"We can do this, Neena," I say gently. "Maybe you dreamweaving flowers or cream buns alone won't be enough. But we're a team, remember? I can help you. The fairies are nature spirits, so let's release them into a field of flowers *so huge* they have no choice but to remember their true selves."

I can't believe I'm the one suggesting we release hundreds of ravenous fairies loose in Neena's dream, but I've survived a nightmare alone *and* been chased by a pack of scary fairies. If I'm not brave, then I don't know who is.

Neena looks up at me and wipes the tears from her cheeks. Her nose is still a bit snotty but I pretend not to notice.

"OK. I trust you, Tito. Let's do this."

Together we run away from the fairy net and into a clearing on the side of the valley where there's more free land. Neena holds my hands and after a quick nod of understanding, we close our eyes.

I imagine my mind like a clear sky, brushing away any thoughts that try to pop in. I can feel Neena's hands become warm and buzz with energy, so I focus on mine. I imagine energy, like heatwaves, pouring out of them. I feel the air around us change so I open my eyes and see wobbling wavy lines completely surrounding us in a bubble. The world around us looks rippling and alive.

Neena nods at me once again and I know it's time to start dreamweaving.

I will the ground around me to start producing flowers. Big, beautiful blooms in every different colour, just like Mama's flower patch in summertime.

Then, one by one, sprouts begin pushing up from the earth. Green shoots grow all around us, filling the clearing where we stand. Petals appear from the quickly growing stems in all colours of the rainbow. As they pop open in a cloud of white dust, I can't believe my eyes.

"Pastries!?"

In the middle of each flower head is a perfect pastry! Chocolate eclairs, doughnuts, cinnamon buns, even *cannolis* like my nonna makes. They sit in the middle of each flower looking delicious and strange all at once.

"I thought we were weaving flowers?" I say in shock.

"I did too, but maybe I still had the cream fingers on my mind..." Neena replies, her eyes wide.

We burst out laughing. I step forwards and accidentally squash a custard-tart carnation which just makes us laugh even harder. I try to get a hold of myself; we still have a job to do.

"I think this will work even better," I say, surveying the field. "It's time to release the fairies."

"I'm on it," Neena says, focusing on the tree where the fairies are held captive in their net. I watch her concentrate as a huge pair of scissors appear in mid-air above the net and with one movement, snip it wide open.

We dive behind some shrubbery to take cover and watch as the fairies swarm out, pooling into the field of pastry flowers. They begin absolutely ravaging the goods, tearing apart choux buns like lions feasting on a gazelle. It's carnage but I can't look away.

"Is it working?" I ask Neena. "I can't tell."

Neena stays quiet for a while, not moving a muscle as she watches the fairies' progress. Suddenly she points at a group of fairies to the left of us, gobbling some apple turnovers.

"Look at them!" she whispers excitedly. "They're turning back to their normal colour."

I watch as the fairies' skin morphs from shocking red to a pale, milky yellow. Their hair relaxes back into loose flowing curls and their eyes become round and black.

"Look over there!" Neena says again. "And there!"

All around us the fairies begin losing their scary appearance. The horrible red that had filled the field before is now dotted with

glowing
purple,
yellow, blue,
gold and
silver. Their
frantic feasting
slows down
and the fairies
instead begin
gently floating from
one flower to the next,
appraising the damage done
to the pastries. I look closely at their faces:
a tiny button nose, big eyes like a bug and a
small mouth. They're actually quite cute.

"I think they're confused," I whisper,
looking at the expressions on their faces.
"We should talk to them."

Slowly, so we don't frighten them, Neena
and I emerge from the bushes. We make our
way to the middle of the field and as the

fairies start to notice us, they float over.
A small golden fairy flies into the air and
hovers by Neena's face.

"Humans, we were under a spell,
It made us ill, we were not well."

Neena holds out her hand and the fairy
lands gently on it.

"The Bhoot controlled us and sent us
here,
To find you, Neena, and spread his fear,
He made us try to change your hearts,
We did not mean to cause you harm."

I come closer to the fairy and clear my
throat. I'm ready to try out my rhyming skills
too!

"Do not worry, little fairy,
But now you need to leave this place.
The Bhoot could try again to find you,
Run away to somewhere safe."

The fairy looks at me and blinks a few times.
OK, I know that didn't rhyme *completely*

but surely they get the idea!

After a few seconds the fairy nods in understanding, before turning to the field of tiny figures. All at once, the fairies rise into the air, filling it like a thousand tiny stars.

Then, moving as one, they bow in thanks, their wings shimmering with light.

I feel tears spring to my eyes and let them roll down my cheeks, rather than try to hide them. If being sensitivo means I can be a Dreamweaver, then I'm happy to be a softie.

The fairies swirl up high into the sky and round in a circle, creating a portal. Then they slip through and away into a hidden place where I hope the Bhoot will never be able to find them.

Neena sighs as the portal closes and looks back at the field filled with half-eaten pastries.

"I'll have to update the Jinncyclopedia

– 'paris love pastries'. Now what are we supposed to do with all these leftover sweets?" she says, smiling slightly. But the small wrinkle in between her eyebrows tells me that she's worried. She's thinking about her uncle. To be honest, I am too.

I bend to the floor and pick up a particularly big, cream-filled pie. "I think I have an idea what we could do with them…"

Neena's eyes grow wide in understanding.

"Uh, no, no, no!" she shouts, starting to run away.

But I chase after her and launch the pie as hard as I can! It lands, *splat*, right on her head.

"You will pay for that!" Neena yells, stooping down to pick up a pastry.

I scream and run off, feeling a croissant whizz past my head. We duck and dive, laughing and yelping at the same time,

in the biggest food fight ever. All worries
of the Bhoot are forgotten for now.

I grin to myself.

The power of pastry, I guess.

Pari (puh-ree)

English name: fairy

Appearance: small, between 30-40 cm in height,
slim limbs and long torso, colours can include any in
the rainbow, but most tend to be a single solid colour.
Hair is loose and flowing, eyes are large, round and
entirely black.

Behaviour: playful, can be mischievous, nimble,
always travel in groups.

Likes: nature, flowers, trees, shrubbery, riddles and
rhymes, food (especially sweet food) Pastries are a hit.

Sightings in dreams:
Tirich Mir, Hindu Kush mountain range
Lower Himalayas
Chitral valley
South coast, UK.

Notable sightings:

1932 - Dreamweaver Abdullah Mirza encountered a green-and-blue streaked pari while dreaming on the Tirich Mir mountain.

1974 - Dreamweaver Aisha encountered a troupe of water paris while dreaming on a boat travelling the Indus River.

2023 - Dreamweavers Neena and Tito broke the spell enchanting a horde of paris and sent them to hide from further danger.

CHAPTER TEN
BACK TO NORMAL?

I want to say that everything has gone back to normal but it hasn't. Roberto is eating his vegetables and *enjoying* them.

Mama has cut up some cucumber and carrots for his breakfast and, to our surprise, Berto is happily munching on them.

"Mmm," he says, dribbling. "Carrots."

It's even weirder than seeing a bird with a moustache or a singing hot dog.

"Mama, can I ask you a question?" I say, eating my cereal.

Mama turns from the stove where she's

pouring coffee. "Of course, but ask in Italiano."

I sigh and search for the right words in my head. "Perché sono sensitivo?" Why am I sensitive?

Mama smiles and comes to sit down at the table. "Oh, Tito. Ever since you were a baby, we knew exactly what you were feeling. You felt every emotion so strongly. When you were happy, you were the happiest baby on earth. When you were angry, oh, you let us know." Mama laughs. "But when you grew up, we knew you also understood other people's emotions very well too. You always know what other people are feeling. In Italiano we have another word that means sensitive – sensibile."

I nod. Mama has spoken to me in Italian since I was a baby.

"But I choose to say sensitivo because it has another meaning. Yes, it means sensitive. But it also means psychic. I think you are sensitive to the things most people cannot see or feel."

I almost choke on my cereal. Does Mama know I'm a Dreamweaver? No, she can't possibly. I look up at her and she is smiling at me over her tiny cup of coffee.

"And you've always been brave – you have to be when you're sensitivo. You feel all those emotions so strongly but forge ahead anyway on your own path. You must get that from me." Mama winks and kisses me on the head.

The back door creaks open and Mum pops her head in, her welder's goggles perched on top of her forehead. "Tito, my boy, time for school," she says.

I kiss Mama and Berto goodbye, gather up my school bag and head out into the garden. It's a cold morning but the sun is shining. Rupert is lying in a small patch of light on the grass and I give him a quick stroke as I pass by. He helped me feel brave last night just by keeping me company.

As we drive to school I keep everything crossed that our plan worked. Will everyone be back to normal?

Will Tiffany and Murray be OK?

★

The first thing I see when I walk in to registration are two rainbow ribbons in Tiffany's pigtail bunches. I'm so happy that I dash forwards and hug her tightly.

"Oooof! You're going to squeeze me to death!" Tiffany laughs, hugging me back.

"I've never been so happy to see ribbons in my life," I squeal. Then I turn to Murray sitting next to Tiff and look him up and down.

Rugby shirt? Check. P.E. shorts? Check. Puffer jacket? Gone.

"You don't feel like singing, do you?" I say cautiously.

"Absolutely not. I am tone-deaf," Murray says, his usual blunt self once more. "I will never sing or dance again."

I sigh and flop into my chair with relief. We did it! We really broke the spell!

Neena appears at the classroom door, her eyes narrowed at Murray and Tiffany.

"You aren't arguing any more?" she says cautiously, walking over to our desk.

Tiffany shakes her head vigorously. "Nope, I'm a lover not a fighter. Sorry about that, Neena, not a great first impression of us."

"Don't worry about it, I'm just glad you're

175

back to your normal selves." Neena smiles. Tiffany jumps up and gives her a hug and my heart feels like it could burst.

"I'm glad we're back to normal too," Murray says, his eyes wide. "I don't know what happened to me. My mum said it was 'hormones' whatever that means. I'm just glad to be back in my rugby kit. Though I can't find my socks anywhere…"

"All great pop stars experiment with their style," Tiffany flicks a pigtail. "But athletic wear is not for me."

I notice that Murray is looking at me strangely. "You know, I think you were in my dream last night, Tito… You too, Neena."

I hold my breath and try to act casual.

"But then I did eat cheese before bed, which gives me trapped wind and strange dreams," Murray says. "I can never remember my dreams properly anyway."

I let out a sigh of relief and look at the rest of our class. Everyone's chatting happily, including Leonard and Harry who are doing some extra homework before the day starts.

"Tito," Neena whispers when Murray and Tiffany aren't paying attention. "Can you come to my house after school? I would like to introduce you to my mum and grandma."

I feel a little flurry of nerves in my stomach. Go to Neena's house and meet her family? That sounds exciting and scary all at the same time.

"I'll call my mum at lunch and ask. But I'm sure she'll say yes," I reply. "Will your mum mind me coming over, though?"

"Of course not. In fact, she's the one who asked."

★

At 3.05 p.m. we wave to Murray and Tiffany, promising to go and play at the park tomorrow after school. I'm looking forward to all of us hanging out together. Three was a good number, but four is a proper group.

We walk round the side of the park to the street where Neena lives. We reach the house at the end of the row and Neena opens a small iron gate that leads into the front garden. I can smell something delicious cooking. Before I can ask Neena what the amazing smell is, the front door opens and a woman stands in the doorway.

"Welcome, Tito. I'm Neena's mum – we've been so excited to meet you," she says in a warm voice. I notice she has the same bright green eyes as Neena. The same as the Bhoot.

"I'm happy to meet you too," I say back, feeling a bit shy.

"Come in, please. My name is Ameena."

As I walk into the narrow corridor, I can hear pots and pans hissing steam from the kitchen. I follow Ameena through to the back of the house and into a cosy living room.

Sitting in a wrinkled leather armchair is an old lady. Her hair is white and tied back into a little bun, revealing large brown eyes. She smiles when she sees me and Neena.

"Neena!" she calls, holding her arms out weakly.

Neena runs up to her grandma and speaks to her in their language. I can tell that Neena is introducing me so I hold up my hand and do a little wave.

There's a door at the back of the living room that leads into the garden. Ameena joins us in the living room and opens it, despite the chilly weather. "Leave your jacket on, Tito. It's cold out there."

I stand still in the living room, confused, as I watch Neena and her family go outside. I assume I'm supposed to follow so I hurry along after them.

In the middle of the patio is a small fire in an iron bowl. There are four woven mats around it, one of which has some cushions on.

"Tito, come sit next to me," Neena says, patting the mat next to her. "It's warmer in front of the fire."

When everyone's settled down, Ameena starts speaking. "I know this must seem a little strange, Tito."

I keep my mouth shut so I don't say anything silly.

"But now you are a Soothsayer too,

we want to initiate you properly," Ameena explains. "We welcome you to our community."

The fire dances in front of me and I watch the heatwaves. They look like the ones that appear when we're dreamweaving.

"So you're Dreamweavers as well?" I ask, looking to Ameena and Neena's grandma.

"Nope! My mum can read the stars to tell the future!" Neena jumps in, beaming with pride. "And my grandma is a healer."

I look at the women with wonder. It feels very special to be part of the same community as them.

"We're so pleased that you are a Dreamweaver. And I know my daughter will teach you everything you need to know." Ameena opens a little wooden box sitting next to her on the mat. "Stay on the path of good and stick together. Who knows when my brother Rahim will return…"

I can see sadness in Ameena's eyes.
She takes something that looks like tea
leaves from the box and throws them on
to the fire. They send out little sparks as
they fizz and burn, along with a woody
scent.

Then she passes the box to her mother,
who takes a handful of leaves from it.
She chants something in Khowar and

then tosses the dried leaves on to the flames.
Neena is next. She takes a handful of leaves
and says, "The path of good." Then she
throws them on to the fire and passes it
to me.

I take the box, not quite knowing what
I'm supposed to say or do.

I take a handful of the dried leaves and
copy Neena. "The path of good."

But then the strong smell of the leaves gets
up my nose and it tickles –

"ACHOO!"

I sneeze the leaves right out of my hands
and into the flames!

I feel heat rising in my cheeks. Trust me to
ruin the serious moment!

But when I look up Neena and her mum
are smiling, and her grandma is slapping her
thigh in laughter.

"Now you're initiated, you take on the joys
and responsibilities of being a Soothsayer,"

Ameena continues. "The Bhoot must still be in Pakistan. From what you've told me, it sounds like he has formed an alliance with other Darkweavers. They will be sticking together as their power is strongest as a group."

"Do you think …" Neena asks quietly, "they will try to control more jinn?"

Ameena's expression darkens. "I do not know. But you must teach Tito all you can, and quickly, to prepare him just in case. I fear this isn't the last we've seen of the Bhoot and his alliance."

"But why does he want *me*?" Neena asks. "He knows I don't want to become a Darkweaver."

I know the answer to this one.

"Neena, I've seen you create portals as large as swimming pools, and make huge silver wings without even thinking about it. You're powerful – maybe more than you even know." I shake my head. "But the Bhoot taught you how to Dreamweave… If anyone knows the potential of your powers, it's him."

Neena and Ameena sit in silence for a while.

"I think you're right," Ameena finally says. "And who knows what he could have planned."

More attacks from jinn? Chaos in the spirit world? I dread to think of the possibilities. But I also know something for sure. I feel it, strong and certain in my heart.

"We're a team – the Dream Team." I stand up and look into the fire. "We'll stop the Bhoot and ensure the spirit world and the human world are safe. Together."

Neena stands up next to me and takes my hand. Her green eyes blaze. "Together."

JOIN THE DREAM TEAM IN
THEIR NEXT ADVENTURE...

DREAM WEAVERS

ROAR OF THE HUNGRY BEAST

COMING FEBRUARY 2024!

ABOUT THE AUTHOR

Annabelle Sami is a writer and arts producer living in London. She writes diverse mystery stories and 'anarchically silly fun' (Guardian) comedy books for children. Her book *Llama Out Loud* was shortlisted for the Waterstones Children's Book Prize, who wrote, 'Sami constructs her story with flawless comic timing' and won the Spark! Book Award 2020. Annabelle's mission in all her work is to give funny, smart and adventurous children of colour, characters they can relate to.

ABOUT THE ILLUSTRATOR

Forrest Burdett is an illustrator
from New Jersey with an eye for whimsy,
a heart full of magic, and a passion for
vibrant colours. He studied Illustration
at the Fashion Institute of Technology
and now lives in Portland, Oregon.
He loves finding magic in the small,
everyday moments and uses his art as
a means to explore and share them.
You can find more of his work at
forrestburdett.com